"You were involved in a shooting tonight?" Dex asked.

He wrapped his arms around Melissa, his heart racing. Although he hadn't seen her in years, he'd never forgotten how wonderful she felt in his arms. He stroked her back and inhaled the fragrance of rose water, the fragrance that had taunted him in his sleep every day since they'd parted ways.

His nights had been filled with dreams of her to the point that he'd thought he'd never get over her.

Melissa's face paled, and she pulled back and wrapped her arms around her waist as if to hold herself together. He wanted to draw her back into his arms.

But if he did, he might never let go.

Something he'd have to do. He'd walked away from her before because she deserved better.

She still did.

HOSTAGE AT HAWK'S LANDING

USA TODAY Bestselling Author

RITA HERRON

HARLEQUIN INTRIGUE®

To my fabulous daughter Elizabeth for always loving and helping others.

Love you, girl.

Mom

ISBN-13: 978-1-335-60421-7

Hostage at Hawk's Landing

Copyright © 2019 by Rita B. Herron

Recycling programs for this product may not exist in your area.

Printed in U.S.A.

™ www.Harlequin.com

USA TODAY bestselling author **Rita Herron** wrote her first book when she was twelve but didn't think real people grew up to be writers. Now she writes so she doesn't have to get a real job. A former kindergarten teacher and workshop leader, she traded storytelling to kids for writing romance, and now she writes romantic comedies and romantic suspense. Rita lives in Georgia with her family. She loves to hear from readers, so please visit her website, ritaherron.com.

Books by Rita Herron

Harlequin Intrigue

Badge of Justice

Redemption at Hawk's Landing
Safe at Hawk's Landing
Hideaway at Hawk's Landing
Hostage at Hawk's Landing

The Heroes of Horseshoe Creek

Lock, Stock and McCullen
McCullen's Secret Son
Roping Ray McCullen
Warrior Son
The Missing McCullen
The Last McCullen

Cold Case at Camden Crossing
Cold Case at Carlton's Canyon
Cold Case at Cobra Creek
Cold Case in Cherokee Crossing

Visit the Author Profile page at Harlequin.com.

CAST OF CHARACTERS

Dexter Hawk—He wants answers about his father's death and won't let anyone get in the way...even sexy Melissa Gentry.

Melissa Gentry—With her life in danger, she turns to Dexter for protection. But Dex poses a different kind of danger...

Jim Smith—He has no idea who he is, only that someone wants him dead.

Clark McTruitt—Why was this PI after Jim Smith?

Emmet Wilson—Does this expert cattle breeder know something about the missing homeless men?

Vance Baxter—Is this rancher getting rich by cheating others?

Frank Lamar—The local cop investigating the disappearance of the homeless is Dex's friend and mentor. But has he crossed the line?

Chapter One

"I found your father."

Dexter Hawk tensed. Detective Frank Lamar's words echoed over the phone line as if boomeranging off the mountains.

Steven Hawk had left the family ranch and abandoned Dex and his family eighteen years ago, shortly after they'd lost their sister, Chrissy. No one had heard from him since.

Dex had taken advantage of his PI skills to search for him, and asked his friend Detective Lamar to help. Lamar was several years older than him, but had taken Dex under his wing a long time ago, becoming his mentor.

"Dex?" Detective Lamar asked. "You there?"

Dexter released the breath he was holding. He'd waited a long damn time for this phone call. But judging from the tone of Lamar's voice, the news wasn't what he wanted to hear.

"Yeah. Where is he?" Dex finally asked.

"Briar Creek," Lamar said.

Briar Creek? Only thirty miles from Hawk's Landing. Had he been nearby all this time? Or had he moved around, then decided to finally come home? "Did you talk to him?"

"He's not talking, Dex." A tense second passed, filling Dex's head with dread.

"I'm sorry," Lamar said gruffly.

Sweat beaded on Dex's forehead. His father was dead. Lamar didn't have to say the words. His apology said it all.

Dex heaved a breath, his chest straining for air. "I have to see him."

"You can do that at the morgue," Lamar said. "I've already called an ambulance."

"No, don't move him. I'm coming there." He snagged his keys from the end table and rushed outside to the SUV he'd bought when he'd donated his pickup to the ranch for the hands.

"What happened?" Dex asked as he climbed in and started the engine.

"Looks like an accident. Pickup truck ran off the road." A hesitant pause. "Dex, there's really no reason—"

"I mean it, Lamar. Do not move him," Dex said between clenched teeth. "I'll be there ASAP." He had to see him for himself. Had to know exactly what had happened to the man who he'd once ridden piggyback and who taught him to ride and fish. Had to know why he'd just up and left and never even called. Birthdays and holidays had passed. Years of worry and wondering and…grief.

His phone vibrated from the console. He gave a quick glance. Harrison, his oldest brother. For a brief second he wondered if Lamar had called him, but he'd sworn Lamar to secrecy about his desire to find their father, so he let the call go to voice mail. He wouldn't destroy the peace and happiness his mother and brothers had recently found until he knew for certain that this dead man was his father.

His family had no idea he'd made it his mission to find him. Not that he had some wild fantasy about a happy reunion with their long-lost patriarch, but Dex's anger had festered for years. He'd practiced what he'd say to his old man for so long that disappointment swamped him.

Now he wouldn't even get the pleasure of telling him off.

Memories of his childhood bombarded him as he drove. His father playing horseshoes with him and his brothers in the backyard. The camping trip where they'd told ghost stories while they huddled in their tent to escape the rain. His father teaching him how to tie knots and rope cattle.

He turned onto a side road that wove past farmland and neared the small town of Briarwood. Briar Creek was known for flooding during heavy storms, but the land looked dry now, and the water low.

He spotted Lamar's unmarked police car on the side of the road around a curve, an ambulance behind it. He parked a few feet behind the ambulance, then climbed out, the summer heat oppressive. Dusk was settling in, the sun was fading and gray clouds were adding a dismal feel.

A drop-off on the left side led from the shoulder of the road to the creek. A black, rusted pickup had nose-dived into the water.

Gravel skittered beneath his boots as he descended the hill and approached it. Lamar was speaking to the medics, his craggy face beaded with perspiration. When he looked up at Dex, his expression was grim.

"We're ready to move him," Lamar said.

Dex held up a hand. "Just give me a minute." He swallowed hard. "Please."

A heartbeat passed before Lamar replied. "All right. Just don't touch anything."

Dex hiked over to the truck with Lamar on his heels. The front of the pickup was submerged in about six inches of water, the passenger door ajar. The driver was slumped forward, his head against the steering wheel. The scent of whiskey assaulted Dex, obviously from the empty liquor bottle on the seat.

Disgust slammed into Dex. Had his father turned into a drunk?

With gloved hands, Lamar lifted the man's head away from the steering wheel. Blood streaked his face and arms, his nose was crushed, and a jagged scar ran along the upper right side of his forehead. Gray streaked the man's shaggy hair and beard.

Dex inhaled a deep breath. He hadn't seen his father in eighteen years. Anger and resentment had obliterated memories and images of him until he had a hard time picturing him in his mind.

He remembered that he was a big man, and this man was big. Was he looking at him now?

He cleared his throat, forcing back emotions. He was a PI; he had answers to find. "What made you certain this is my father?"

Lamar rubbed a hand over his sweaty face, then lifted a bag holding an ID. Dexter peered at the ID through the plastic. The name on the driver's license was Steven Hawk.

"I found these in the dash, too." Lamar held up another evidence bag, and Dex's chest tightened. Photos. One of him and his brothers and sister when they were little, then another of his father and mother on their wedding day. His mother still kept the same picture on her dresser in her bedroom.

"I'm sorry, Dex," Lamar said.

Dex blinked hard. He damn well would not cry, not in front of Lamar. And not for the man who'd walked out on him and his family and never looked back.

But denial also reared its ugly head. "I want DNA for confirmation."

"Of course," Lamar said.

Dex studied the dead man's features, struggling to make this bloody face belong to the man he'd loved and idolized.

But an image of his father laughing when Dex had fallen from his horse into a mud puddle surfaced and moisture blurred his eyes. A second later, he saw his father's strained expression as he searched the woods for Chrissy, then the anger in his eyes when the sheriff had treated him like a suspect. But it was his mother's tearstained cheeks the morning after his father hadn't come home that still haunted him.

That was the final blow that had nearly crushed her.

Lamar waved the medics down the hill to remove the body from the truck. Dex noticed a business card on the floor by the seat, snatched the card and jammed it in his pocket. Maybe something on the card would lead him to answer the questions that kept him awake at night. Like where his father had been all this time.

Had he forgotten about his family? Found happiness with another woman?

Had he even thought about them?

Emotions pummeling him, he turned and strode back up the hill. Lamar would let him know when the DNA results were in. Then he'd have to break the news to his family.

Not tonight, though. Tonight he'd grieve alone.

He fingered the card in his pocket as he climbed in his SUV and pulled out the wooden nickel he always carried.

His father's voice echoed in his head. "Don't take any wooden nickels, son."

Dex had taken that meaning to heart. He'd never accepted anything at face value and always investigated things himself.

The name of a homeless shelter had been scrawled on the card.

Maybe someone there could tell him more about his father.

Six weeks later

MELISSA GENTRY SIPPED HER evening tea as she ducked into her small office at the Lend-A-Hand Shelter outside Austin. The evening meal was complete. Tonight the volunteers had served over a hundred dinners, shared stories and camaraderie with the transients who'd wandered in and passed out personal hygienic supplies and water bottles to everyone who'd shown up. The summer heat was stifling, the danger of heat stroke and dehydration always high during the summer months.

The staff was busy clearing the dishes and cleaning the kitchen, while a few of the short-term residents who'd committed to a plan to get back on their feet gathered in the common room for a game of cards.

She glanced at the newspaper as she took her break, her heart clenching. The Hawk family was back in the news. Last year, they'd found their long-lost sister's body, tying up the mystery of what had happened to Chrissy Hawk nearly two decades ago.

Then a few months ago, a human trafficking ring had struck Tumbleweed, drawing the attention of the FBI and brother Lucas Hawk. The head of the ring had forced a local plastic surgeon to change his face so he could create a new identity, and lawyer brother Brayden Hawk had helped the feds take down the trafficking ring.

But her attention was focused on the photograph and current headline. Dexter Hawk, the third brother, and the man who'd stolen her heart her first year of college, stood by a grave with his family as they said goodbye to Steven Hawk, his father who'd disappeared shortly after his daughter had.

Some had speculated that he'd run off because he'd hurt Chrissy, but that theory had been rectified when the family learned that Chrissy had been killed by a man with a developmental disability. The more likely scenario for the father's abandonment was that guilt and grief had eaten at him until he'd left. Couples rarely survived the loss of a child.

Sympathy and envy swelled in her chest. That family had suffered so much, yet they stood together in loving support by Mr. Hawk's grave.

All her life, she'd craved a family like that. But working at the shelter had taught her that you had to play the cards you'd been dealt in life. So she'd made a family with the volunteers and the drifters who wandered in for food and comfort and a helping hand.

Voices and noises echoed from the front, the sound of arguing forcing her to leave the privacy of the office. She walked down the hall, then poked her head into the doorway of the gathering room to assess the situation.

While she empathized with those in need, instincts warned her to stay alert for trouble. Some people fell on hard times and were humble and wanted help. Others suffered from mental issues, drug addictions and PTSD. There were also criminals who took refuge in shelters and on the streets to escape the law.

She stole a look at the man who'd joined them a few days ago. Jim Smith. He was quiet and secretive, and kept to himself. The dark intensity in his expression suggested something was wrong, that he was on the run from something—or somebody.

She and April Stewart, the director of the shelter, had discussed consulting the local police, but Smith had given them no reason to. If they called the cops on everyone who made them nervous, they might as well shut down.

On the surface, Smith looked rough. He had a long scar on the side of his face, walked with a limp and he was missing the end of the third finger on his left hand. But he'd been polite and respectful to her and April. They'd encouraged him to share his story, but so far he hadn't opened up.

He didn't appear to be mentally ill or an addict. Perhaps he'd recently lost a loved one or his family. Deep grief often forced people to retreat into depression to the point of losing their homes.

Two of the men at the card table were squabbling,

one of them accusing the other of stealing his King of Hearts. Smith stepped in, calming them both by clarifying that the card was on the floor.

Melissa smiled. Sometimes Jim surprised her by showing a softer side. It made her even more curious about his background and how he'd ended up at Lend-A-Hand.

She cradled her tea mug in her hands as she bypassed the kitchen and made her way to the common room.

The card game ended, and a few of the men headed outside to wherever they wanted to go for the night, while others retreated to the bunk room. The kitchen volunteers waved good-night and hurried out the back door. Smith grabbed a cup of coffee, sat down at the table and started scribbling something in a small notepad, which, she'd noticed, he did a lot. She wondered what he was writing.

She locked the front door, but a noise from the back made her jerk around, and she rushed to make sure one of the volunteers hadn't returned and needed her. Or it could be Samuel, the night volunteer arriving.

But just as she reached the hallway, the door to the back burst open. Melissa startled and called out Samuel's name, but a man in dark clothes and a mask grabbed her and shoved a gun to her head.

She opened her mouth to scream, but the man tightened his hold around her throat. "We don't have money or drugs," she managed to say in a choked whisper.

"Shut up." He shoved her forward, and she stumbled and bumped the corner of the wall. He pushed her harder, his voice a growl in her ear. "Where is he?"

Fear clawed at Melissa. "Who?"

"Smith," the man snapped.

"I'm right here."

Melissa's eyes widened as Smith stepped into the doorway, his hands held up in surrender. His dark brown eyes met hers, worry and an apology that she didn't understand etched in the depths.

Then Smith shot an angry look at the gunman. "Let her go and I'll do whatever you want."

Chapter Two

Melissa clenched her jaw. She didn't know why this gunman wanted Jim, but her protective instincts for the drifters at the shelter kicked in. She'd taken self-defense classes, and was tempted to jab her elbow into the man's stomach, then jerk his arm up so hopefully he'd drop the gun. But common sense warned her that if she made a mistake, she'd end up dead and so might Jim Smith.

She couldn't live with his death on her conscience.

The brute with the gun tightened his hold, the gun barrel pressing against her temple. "You'd better back off, Smith, or the little lady gets it."

Tension radiated from Jim's body as he went ram-rod still. "It's me you want. Let her go and we'll take this outside."

The man shook his head and shoved her toward a chair in the corner. "Tie her up, then we talk."

Melissa bit her lip to keep from crying out as she sank into the metal folding chair. As much as she wanted to fight, she had to consider the other men in the back. The intruder pulled a rope from his pocket and tossed it toward Jim. He snatched it, then shocked her by swinging it like a cowboy and throwing it toward

the gunman like a lasso. The movement caught the gunman off guard, and Jim charged the brute.

The man grunted and the two of them slammed
against the wall as they wrestled for the gun. Footsteps
sounded from the back, and two of the homeless men,
Gunther and Dwayne, rushed into the doorway. She
shouted for them to stay back.

Jim threw the intruder to the floor and jerked the
man's arm up. The weapon went off, the bullet hitting the
ceiling. Jim knocked the gun from the man's hand, and
it skidded across the floor. Melissa ran for the weapon,
but the shooter snagged her leg as she passed him. She
tripped and went down hard, her knee slamming into
the wood floor.

Jim rolled twice, then reached the gun and snatched
it. The brute jumped him, and they struggled, but the
gun went off again. Melissa covered her mouth to sti-
fle a scream as the gunman collapsed on top of Jim.

Was Jim hurt?

A second later, he shoved his attacker off him. Blood
oozed from the gunman's chest, and he made a choking sound, then gurgled blood.

Jim pushed himself to stand, the gun in his hands,
the other man's blood soaking his shirt. The shooter's
body jerked and spasmed, then he suddenly stilled,
eyes wide and blank.

Jim looked over at her, his jaw clenched. "Are you
all right?"

She nodded, too stunned to speak. He gestured toward Gunther. "Call 9-1-1."

Gunther nodded and rushed toward the phone the
men were allowed to use on the counter in the corner.

Melissa swallowed, and struggled to stand on shaky legs. She had to know why the man wanted Jim.

But he jammed the pistol into the back of his jeans and ran for the side door. "I'm sorry, Melissa," he murmured, then he unlocked the door and disappeared.

Outside, a siren wailed. The police. Jim had left just in time to avoid them. Why? She would have vouched that he'd acted in self-defense.

And that he'd saved her life.

Dex climbed in his SUV and flipped on the radio as he left the homeless shelter near Tumbleweed. Damn. Another drifter had gone missing. That was three in recent months.

The director had reiterated what he'd heard at the two other places he'd visited: the homeless who took refuge at the shelters didn't stay long. The center had no control over where the men went and rarely was informed of their destinations when they left.

Worse, none of the men wanted to talk to him. They seemed wary, even suspicious of his intentions. He'd tried to assure them that he was concerned that someone might be preying on transients, but the only thing he'd accomplished was planting fear in the men's eyes.

Grief still made his chest ache. The damn DNA had confirmed that the man found at Briar Creek was his father. He and his family had mourned and buried him beside Chrissy.

But questions over where his father had been and what he'd been doing for eighteen years gnawed at him. What had happened to drive him to alcohol and the streets? Chrissy's disappearance had been horrible for all of them. But his mother hadn't walked out on her sons or buried herself in a bottle.

Had his father seen the news about Chrissy's body being found, and been driven over the edge by grief?

Dammit, there was nothing he could do to bring his father back. But in his search for answers, he'd stumbled on another mystery.

Even if his father's death wasn't connected to the other missing men, Dex was determined to make sure a predator wasn't taking advantage of these homeless men when they were already down. If nothing else, he'd find the truth in honor of his father.

A newscast broke into the country music on the radio as he headed toward the small apartment he rented over his PI office in Austin.

"This late breaking story just in. A man was shot and killed tonight at the Lend-A-Hand Shelter outside Austin. Assistant Director Melissa Gentry stated that a gunman broke into the facility just as the shelter was locking up for the night and held her at gunpoint. According to Ms. Gentry, one of the men at the shelter jumped the gunman to defend her, and the gun went off. The gunman died on-site, then the other man disappeared."

Dex's heart pounded. Melissa Gentry. Her name was a blast from the past. A blast of happy memories and a time when he'd allowed himself to enjoy the company of a good woman. Although when he'd found himself falling in love with her, he'd broken it off. Well, technically he hadn't exactly done that. He'd walked away like a coward.

Maybe he was like his old man...

Melissa was sweetness and kindness and way too damn good for the likes of him.

He'd known that she'd wanted to be a social worker, so hearing about her job at Lend-A-Hand fit.

The reporter segued to another story, and he veered to the side of the road, plugged the name Lend-A-Hand Shelter into his GPS, then pulled back into traffic and drove toward it.

The thought of a man holding a gun to Melissa made his blood turn cold. He wanted to see for himself that she wasn't harmed. And if she knew anything about the other missing transient men.

If someone was targeting them, tonight's shooting might be connected.

MELISSA WAS STILL trembling as the police roped off the shelter as a crime scene. Detective Frank Lamar from the Austin PD was in charge, delegating a female cop named Nikki Whalen to question the men at the shelter. Melissa could barely control her anger. These men had fallen on hard times, yet now they were being treated as suspects.

She'd given her statement. Told the truth. Assured the detective that none of the other men were involved in the shooting incident, but he'd quickly silenced her with a warning to let him do his job.

Questions about Jim Smith needled her. If he wasn't hiding from the law, why had he run?

A noise from the front door jarred her from her thoughts. Detective Lamar strode to the door to speak to the officer in charge of securing the scene.

"What's going on, Frank?"

Melissa paused to listen. A male voice. Angry? Concerned?

"I want to talk to Melissa."

Melissa tensed. The man…his voice sounded familiar. She hadn't heard it in ages, but…it sounded like Dexter Hawk.

"This is a crime scene. I can't let you come in," Detective Lamar said bluntly.

Melissa hurried to the door and nudged up beside the stocky cop. He was about her height, but his voice and demeanor were intimidating. By design, probably.

"Melissa?"

Her heart pounded. It *was* Dexter.

"Dex?"

The cop looked back and forth between them, his bushy eyebrows furrowed. "You two know each other?"

"Yes," they said at the same time.

"Well, hell." The cop scraped a hand down his chin.

Dex took a step forward. "Lamar, you know I've been investigating the missing transients since we found my father. This incident could be related."

"It's not," the detective said brusquely. "You saw Dr. Hudson's autopsy report. Your father's death was an accident, Dex. Accept it and move on."

"I wish we could have used Dr. Weinberger from Tumbleweed," Dex said. "I know him and trust him."

"Hudson is a good ME," Lamar said.

Melissa twisted her hands by her sides. Apparently Dex and this detective knew each other, too. PI to cop, or were they friends?

"Go home, Dex, and let me handle this," Detective Lamar said.

Melissa made a snap decision. She hadn't seen Dex in almost ten years. She wanted to tell him how sorry she was about his father. To ask him why he thought his father's death, the missing transients and the shooting might be connected.

"Excuse me, Detective," she said, giving the cop a gentle push as she reached for the door. "I need some air."

He started to protest, but she slanted him an icy look. Ever since he'd arrived at the shelter, he'd made her and the residents feel as if they'd done something wrong. "You can't make me stay inside," she said simply. "Not unless you're going to charge me with something."

The man's thick lips pressed into a tight line. A breath laced with the foul scent of cigarettes wheezed out, then he stepped aside. "Just don't leave the county without telling me," he said. "I might need to ask you some more questions."

She gave a quick nod, then pushed past him and out the door. The odor of blood and death inside the shelter was making her nauseous.

She quickly dragged in a breath, then looked up to see Dex's handsome face. Worry darkened the depths of his eyes as he gently took her arm and led her down the steps to a cluster of trees. She was still shaking so badly that her legs nearly buckled.

"Ahh, Melissa." A second later, Dexter pulled her up against him, and she leaned her head into his chest.

DEXTER WRAPPED HIS arms around Melissa, his heart racing. Although he hadn't seen her in years, he'd never forgotten how wonderful she felt in his arms. He stroked her back, and inhaled the fragrance of rosewater, the fragrance that had taunted him in his sleep every day since they'd parted ways.

His nights had been filled with dreams of her to the point that he'd thought he'd never get over her.

She clung to his chest, her shaky breathing doing a number on his emotions.

Maybe he *hadn't* gotten over her. He sure as hell hadn't let any other woman in his life or heart since. No…he'd been too damn afraid of loving to put himself out there and chance getting hurt. Watching the heartbreak his mother had suffered when his father left had taught him a lesson.

He hadn't deserved Melissa anyway. Not after he'd told his sister to get lost that night. And then she had. *Forever.*

Still, he couldn't help himself. He rubbed Melissa's back again, savoring the feel of her in his arms for another minute. She was alive. She appeared unharmed, at least physically.

Time to do his job and talk. Not lose himself traipsing down memory lane.

"You okay, darlin'?"

She nodded against him and gave a deep sigh. "Thanks." She patted his chest, then eased from his embrace and lifted her chin. "Sorry."

"No apologies," he murmured, his chest squeezing with emotions again. Damn, she had that effect on him. The thought of anyone hurting her made him want to pound something.

He swallowed hard, forcing his mind back on track and his eyes away from her beautiful face. The sight of that unruly dark auburn hair that had driven him mad when he'd run his fingers through it taunted him to touch it again.

He had to resist.

"I saw the story about your father. I'm sorry," she said softly.

Dexter ground his teeth, the pain back. "I want answers," he said honestly.

"He died in an automobile accident?"

He nodded. Thankfully, the paper hadn't revealed that he was inebriated at the time. "I found a card from another homeless shelter in his truck."

She tucked a strand of hair behind one ear, a frown marring her heart-shaped face. "He was living in a shelter?"

"I don't know," Dexter said. "But I've been visiting some of them to see if anyone knew him. I'm curious as to what he was doing all this time." And why he never came back.

Lamar's voice as he spoke to the officer guarding the scene echoed from the front stoop, jerking Dex back to the reason he'd come.

"You were involved in a shooting tonight?" Dex asked.

Her face paled, and she wrapped her arms around her waist as if to hold herself together. He wanted to draw her back into his arms.

But if he did, he might never let go.

Something he'd have to do. He'd walked away from her before because she deserved better.

She still did.

Chapter Three

Melissa rubbed her arms to erase the chill invading her. Dex's warm embrace reminded her of feelings that had never really gone away.

Dex exhaled. "What happened here?"

"We were locking up for the night when this man burst in the back door. He had a gun and grabbed me, said he wanted Jim Smith."

"Did he say why?" Dex asked.

She shook her head. "No, it happened really fast. He pushed me toward the common room, then Jim appeared. Jim offered to trade himself for me, then the gunman told Jim to tie me up. He tossed him a rope. Smith grabbed the rope, then charged the man with the gun."

Detective Lamar stepped outside, his voice carrying in the slight breeze that stirred. "I want an APB out on this man. Name is Jim Smith. Approach with caution. He's already killed one man tonight, and is armed and dangerous."

Melissa tensed at the detective's tone. She crossed the space to him as he hung up. "Detective Lamar," she said. "Jim isn't dangerous, at least not in the way you're suggesting. He acted in self-defense. He wasn't armed when he came here."

Dexter had followed her over to the cop, his arms crossed as he listened.

"How do you know Smith didn't have a gun?" the detective asked. "Did you search his belongings?"

"Well, no," Melissa admitted. "But I didn't see any signs of a weapon. In fact, he was almost gentle at times. He tried to talk the gunman down, then he wrestled with the man and the gun went off." Her voice cracked as the memory returned. "He was a hero, not the enemy. He saved my life." And she wanted to thank him for it, not see him hunted down like an animal.

"You certainly are defensive of him." The detective narrowed his eyes. "Exactly how well did you know Mr. Smith?"

Anger shot through Melissa at the insinuations in the cop's voice. "He was a welcome guest here just like all of the other men who seek housing with us at Lend-A-Hand."

"What was his story?" Detective Lamar asked. "Did he have a family?"

Melissa bit the corner of her lip, a habit she had when thinking. "I don't know. He'd only been here a couple of days and didn't share much about himself."

"What *did* he share?" the detective asked.

Melissa searched her memory banks. "Nothing really. He was quiet, and kept to himself. But he was always polite at mealtimes and respectful of the other men and our volunteers."

"So you're defending a man you know virtually nothing about," Detective Lamar said flatly. "His name sounds fake. He could be a criminal hiding out."

She had considered that. "I don't think that's the case."

Detective Lamar raised a brow. "What *do* you think?"

Dex cleared his throat. "Lamar, why don't you lay off? Melissa told you all she knows. It's her job to help the men who come here, not interrogate them."

Officer Whalen, who'd been questioning the men inside, stepped to the door. "I'm finished here."

The detective shrugged. "You get anything useful?"

Officer Whalen shook her head. "No one seemed to know anything about Smith. General consensus was that he didn't want to talk. One guy thought Smith was hiding something. Another said Smith hinted that he didn't have family. But Smith didn't elaborate so we don't know if he was married, divorced, had kids, or if he did, what happened to them."

"What about a job?" Detective Lamar asked.

The officer shook her head. "Didn't mention one."

The detective turned back to Melissa. "Did he tell you what kind of work he did?"

He'd thrown that rope lasso-style, like a pro. Maybe ranching? Then again, most men in Texas knew how to rope and ride. "I'm afraid not." She lifted her chin. "Instead of investigating Smith, why aren't you looking into the dead man on the floor in the shelter? He's the one who broke in here and put a gun to my head."

DEX COULDN'T DRAG his eyes from Melissa and that tangled mass of hair. She had a heart of gold. But was she naive? Was Smith a criminal, using the shelter to hide from the law? Or...perhaps he was in trouble and the gunman was a bad guy chasing him?

Various scenarios bombarded him. Smith might

have owed the man or someone else money. The shooter could have had a personal vendetta against Smith for some transgression against him.

"Listen to me, Ms. Gentry," Lamar said. "We have to close down the shelter until we're finished processing it. The men staying here will have to leave, at least temporarily."

Melissa's eyes flickered with unease. "How long will we have to be closed?"

"I can't say for sure. I'll let you know when we release the space and you can use it again. Meanwhile, I'll have Officer Whalen escort the men outside."

Lamar went to speak to Whalen, and Dex gave Melissa an understanding look. Knowing Melissa, she'd worry about the men they'd have to turn away.

"If you find a place for the men to stay tonight, I'll provide transportation," he offered.

Melissa's look of gratitude suggested he'd read her correctly. She was more concerned about Smith and the men at the shelter than she was about herself. "Thanks, Dex. I will do that. I don't like the idea of putting anyone out when it's so hot."

Melissa removed her phone from the pocket of her jeans and stepped aside to make a phone call.

Lamar walked back to him, his expression grim.

"Don't you think you were a little hard on her?" Dex asked, annoyed at his friend.

"I'm just doing my job." Lamar grunted. "How do you know her?"

Dex didn't intend to share details of their relationship. "We met in college."

"I didn't think you went to college," Lamar said.

Dex gritted his teeth. He had gone but not finished.

Brayden was definitely the most educated of the Hawk men. Still, he loved his work. "I did, but just one semester. College wasn't for me. I did take business classes at a local school though before I hung my shingle."

Lamar worked his mouth from side to side. "I take it you and Ms. Gentry were…involved?"

Dex shrugged. "It was a long time ago. But I can vouch for her. Melissa's the most honest, caring person I've ever met."

"Caring enough that she'd cover for Smith?"

"You heard her story," Dex said. "You can believe her." He gestured toward the inside of the shelter. "Dr. Hudson in there?"

Lamar nodded. "They should be bringing the man's body outside to transport to the morgue any minute."

Dex shoved his hand in his pockets. "What do you know about the gunman?"

"Not much, yet. Name on his ID is Clark McTruitt." Lamar shifted, putting his body between Dex and Melissa as if he didn't want her to overhear what he had to say. "He had a PI license on him, Dex."

A tense minute passed. "He was a PI? Where?" He would recognize his name if he worked out of Austin.

"Amarillo." The door opened and two medics carried a stretcher with McTruitt's body encased in a body bag on it. "He obviously had reason to come after Smith," Lamar said. "Finding out more about Smith is key."

Dex agreed with him on that. "I'll go to McTruitt's office and see what I can dig up."

Lamar's deep frown of disapproval coincided with a firm shake of his head. "Listen, Dex, this is a homicide investigation. I have to play it by the book." He slanted him a warning look. "If I need you, I'll let you know. Otherwise, go home and be with your family, and let me do my job."

Dex clenched his jaw as Melissa strode toward the homeless men being escorted from the shelter. She could have died tonight.

That thought sent fear crawling through him. He didn't give a damn what Lamar said.

There was no way he could walk away without answers.

MELISSA DIDN'T KNOW why the detective rubbed her the wrong way, but he did. She had been defensive of Jim Smith, but rightfully so. Although she had wondered about his past and what he was hiding from, he'd saved her life and she owed him.

She phoned her friend at Another Chance Shelter about forty miles away and explained the situation. The volunteer had enough beds open for the men to stay with them for a few nights if needed.

Several of the men went their own way, although three agreed to move to another facility.

She had a soft spot for Gunther and was glad he accepted the offer. He'd had a hard life. Had been injured in the Gulf War. With a bad leg and PTSD, he'd lost his job when he'd become addicted to pain meds. And he had no family.

An awkward silence filled the car as Dex drove them to the shelter. When they arrived, he parked, climbed out and met her at the passenger side. The men congregated a few feet away, the night taking its toll in the way they spoke in hushed tones about what had happened with the gunman.

"Wait here while I introduce them to the volunteers," Melissa told Dex.

Dex hesitated, shifting on the balls of his feet. "Actually, I wanted to go with you, ask if anyone in there knew my father."

He removed a photo from his wallet. She'd expected to see the picture he'd shown her when they'd met in college, but this photo was of an older man, the one he must have buried.

"Did you ever meet him?" Dex asked.

The pain in his voice ripped at her heartstrings and reminded her that Dex had been lost when they'd first met. She'd wanted to save him, but later realized she couldn't save everyone. She'd learned that with her own father when he'd died with one hand around the bottle, the other holding a pistol.

He hadn't cared enough about her to stick around. That had hurt the most.

Water under the bridge.

She had to move on, do what she could to help others.

She studied the photo, mentally tapping into the decade of homeless men she'd met on the streets or in various shelters, but she didn't recognize the one in the picture. "I'm sorry, Dex, but I don't recall seeing him anywhere." She squeezed his hand, a warmth stirring inside her that triggered emotions she'd once felt for this strong, hurting man.

Dexter clenched his jaw. "All right. But I'd like to ask inside."

She nodded in understanding.

Sadly, she'd heard similar stories from other families before. One family member left, leaving the others full of questions, pain and guilt. God knows she'd had her share of that over her own situation.

It was a complicated problem and could only be dealt with one family at a time.

Heartbreak City, if she let herself get too involved. The reason she needed to keep her distance from Dex. She had her own demons to slay.

And she'd barely survived the first time he'd left her.

She didn't want to revisit that kind of pain again.

DEX JAMMED HIS hands in his pockets. A faint breeze stirred, bringing the scent of cigarette smoke and the hushed voices of the homeless men.

Melissa rolled her shoulders, fatigue showing on her face. "Let's get the men settled."

She texted her friend that she'd arrived, and he followed her to the door. A few minutes later, the men accepted cots in the back of the shelter, and she and Dex stood talking to Edgar, the volunteer.

"I heard what happened," Edgar said with a worried look. "I'm so sorry, Melissa. Are you all right?"

"Yes," Melissa said. "But it's a reminder of how quickly someone can break in."

Dex showed Edgar the recent photograph of his father and another shot of him around the time he'd disappeared.

"I'm sorry, sir," Edgar said. "But he hasn't been here."

"You're sure?" Dex asked.

"Edgar has a near photographic memory," Melissa said.

Dexter eyed the man. He was late forties, wore big chunky brown glasses, had a wide nose and a missing

front tooth. The way he picked at his fingernails indicated nerves, maybe a habit from living a hard life
himself. Everyone had a story.

He just wanted to know what his father's was.

Melissa lapsed into silence as he drove her back
to Lend-A-Hand. When they reached the facility, she
snagged her keys from her purse. "Thanks for driving
us to Another Chance."

"No problem." He spotted a beat-up minivan in the
parking lot and guessed it was hers. Melissa had never
valued material things. "I'll follow you home," he offered.

"That's not necessary." Her voice took on a stiff
ring.

He knew she was shaken, but he wasn't ready to
let her out of his sight. "Melissa, you could have been
hurt tonight." Killed, but he couldn't allow himself to
voice that awful thought aloud. "I'll see that you get
home safely, so don't argue."

Melissa rubbed a hand over her eyes. She was obviously so exhausted she simply nodded and slipped
from his SUV. Just as he thought, the beat-up minivan
belonged to her.

She jammed her keys in the ignition, the engine taking three tries to sputter to life.

Anger that she sacrificed so much for others min-
gled with worry that she might have died doing just
that.

She deserved so much better. To have diamonds
and pearls. At least a car that didn't look as if it had
been rolled twice.

He glanced back at the shelter before he pulled from
the parking lot. Melissa was no doubt worried about

the men she'd had to move tonight. But worry for her raged through him. He didn't like the fact that Melissa put herself in danger by trying to help them. Tonight's incident proved the facility wasn't secure.

The thought of losing her bothered him more than he wanted to admit as he followed her through the streets of Austin. His gut tightened when she veered into an area consisting of transitional homes. A couple had been remodeled, but most looked as if they were teardowns. The street was not in the best part of town, either, and was known for shady activities, including drug rings and gangs.

Her house was a tiny bungalow with a sagging little porch and paint-chipped shutters, and sat next to a rotting shanty where two guys in hoodies hovered by the side porch, heads bent in hushed conversation as if they might be in the middle of a drug deal.

He gritted his teeth as he parked and walked up the graveled path to the front porch. She paused, her key in hand. A handcrafted wreath said Welcome Home, which for some reason twisted his gut even more.

Melissa had never had a real home, while he'd grown up on the ranch with family and brothers and open land.

She offered him a small smile. "Thanks for following me, Dex."

"I'll go in and check the house," he said, itching to make sure that at least her windows and doors were secure. From his vantage point now, it looked as if a stiff wind would blow the house down.

She shook her head. "That's not necessary, but I appreciate it." She ran a shaky hand through her hair. "I'm exhausted. I'm going to bed."

She opened the door and ducked inside without another word and without looking back. An image of her crawling into bed in that lonely old house taunted him.

He wanted to join her. Hold her. Make sure she was all right tonight.

But that would be risky for him.

Still, he couldn't shake the feeling that she was in danger as he walked back to his SUV.

Chapter Four

Melissa closed the door, shutting Dex outside and hoping he left immediately. She had come close to allowing him to come in. But if she had, she might have asked him to stay all night.

And that would be a mistake.

It had taken her months to get over him when he'd walked out of her life in college. She'd dreamed about him for even longer. Worse, she'd compared every date she'd ever had to Dex and no one had come close to measuring up.

Eventually she'd just stopped dating. Had accepted the fact that marriage wasn't for her, that her family was the people she served. They needed her.

Worse tonight…the shelter she'd given so much of her heart and time to was a crime scene.

She dropped her keys and purse on the side table, flipped on the light and scanned the living room. The faded blue couch and rocking chair that had come with the rental house were simple, the walls decorated with a few flea market finds from the owner. Nothing that held any sentimental value to her. And certainly nothing fancy. But she didn't need fancy things.

Just a safe haven to lay her head at night.

Not having personal items made it easier to pack up and move on when she felt the urge.

And she was starting to feel that urge. She'd already been at Lend-A-Hand nearly a year, longer than most places.

Nerves clawed at her stomach. She could have died tonight. And she had watched a man lose his life. She'd seen bad things before, but never death so close-up.

With the temperature soaring outside, she opted for a glass of wine over her cup of nightly hot tea and carried it to the bathroom. She filled the tub with bubble bath, undressed and climbed inside to soak away the stench of blood and death that permeated her skin.

Dex's handsome face flashed behind her eyes. Once they'd shared a bath, had loved each other the way young lovers did.

She wasn't young and innocent anymore, though.

And she couldn't entertain fantasies of Dex again. For all she knew, Dex might be involved with someone else.

She had to focus on work, which made her wonder about Jim Smith. Why had that PI been willing to hold her at gunpoint to get to Jim?

THE NEXT MORNING Dex met his family at the main house for a big country breakfast his mother had prepared. Honey and Harrison and their baby, little Steven, were already there, the baby cooing from the high chair where he banged a spoon on the tray.

Lucas and Charlotte arrived as he did, Lucas steadying a very pregnant Charlotte as they joined the family in the large dining room off the kitchen. Brayden and Mila and Mila's little girl, Izzy, were talking to the foster girls their mother had taken in after they were rescued from the human trafficking ring that Lucas had broken up.

As chatter, laughter and hugs floated between the family members and the ones who'd joined the family, a warmth spread through Dexter. For years after Chrissy disappeared, the family had suffered from guilt and the uncertainty of what had happened to her. Learning she was dead had been a blow, just as learning about their father had been. But at least they had closure.

Love for his family overcame Dex as he thought about Melissa. When they'd dated, she'd confided in him her feelings about losing her mother, about her father moving them from place to place. They'd lived in shelters all her life.

No wonder she was at home there.

It still wasn't fair. She deserved to have more.

"Let's eat," his mother called over the noise.

The next few minutes were hectic as everyone grabbed a plate and served themselves from the buffet. Platters of sausage and bacon, eggs, grits, homemade biscuits and roasted potatoes made Dex's mouth water. One by one, they found seats at the giant farmhouse table the brothers had built to house their growing needs, then his mother tapped her spoon on her coffee mug to indicate it was time for a prayer. The family joined hands and bowed their heads, the voices quieting as their mother gave thanks for all they had.

As the prayer ended, the conversation began again.

The baby squealed as his mother drizzled a biscuit with honey, then tore it into small bites and put it on the tray. Izzy sidled next to the baby and began to talk to him, and the foster girls joined at the opposite end, jabbering about the pool his mother had decided to build so they could cool off in the hot summer.

Charlotte was excited about putting the finishing touches on the nursery for their baby girl who was due any minute. Brayden stood and gestured that he needed everyone's attention.

He motioned for Izzy to join him and Mila, then grinned at Izzy. "You want to tell them, sweetie?"

Izzy bobbed her little head up and down. "I'm gonna be a big sister!"

The family cheered and stood, hugging and congratulating the couple. Dex slapped Brayden on the back. He still couldn't believe his little brother was married and had a stepdaughter. And now he was going to add another child to his new family.

Pulling away, Brayden asked with a grin, "When are you going to settle down, man?"

His mother looked at him, and Dex shrugged. "Not going to let anyone tie me down."

Lucas pounded him on the back. "Because you haven't found the right woman."

Dex chewed the inside of his cheek as an image of Melissa taunted him. She was beautiful and sweet and the most selfless person he'd ever known. She'd invaded his dreams and fantasies since college. She would love his family and would fit right in.

But…losing his sister and father had nearly destroyed him. If he gave his heart to Melissa, she might crush it, too.

So he simply laughed off his brothers' teasing. As they finished breakfast, he asked his brothers to join him in the study. Their mother didn't allow work talk at the table.

Harrison eyed him with a frown. "What's going on, Dex?"

Dex crossed his arms. "Did you hear about the shooting at the Lend-A-Hand Shelter last night?"

"Yeah," Harrison said. "Someone broke in and one of the homeless men shot him."

Lucas pulled a hand down his chin. "Police are looking for the shooter. They suspect he was using an alias, that he was on the run from the law."

Brayden raised an inquisitive brow. "Why are you asking, Dex?"

"I know the woman who runs the shelter," Dex admitted. "Went to college with her years ago."

"You dated her?" Brayden asked.

Dex cursed himself. Why had he shared that he knew her? "Yeah, but that's not the point. She claims Smith wasn't dangerous, that the shooter broke in and put a gun to her head."

Harrison scowled. "What else do you know about Smith?"

"Nothing really," Dex said. "But the shooter was a PI, name was Clark McTruitt."

"Maybe McTruitt knew why Smith was on the run and that he was dangerous."

"But why hold a gun to Melissa?" Dex asked.

"Melissa?" Brayden said with a tease to his voice.

"That's her name," Dex said, irritated. "Anyway, after we found Dad, I asked around at a few shelters to see if anyone had seen him."

"Dex," Lucas said with a warning note to his voice. "Dad abandoned us. No need to ask anything else."

Harrison's jaw tightened. "He's right. You have to let it go."

Brayden twisted his mouth to the side. "Did you find out anything?"

Dex shook his head. "Not yet. But in visiting the shelters, I discovered that three other transients have gone missing the past six months. That started me thinking—"

"That maybe Dad's death wasn't an accident," Brayden said.

Lucas made a sound of disgust. "He was drunk. Loaded, according to the medical examiner's report."

"Transients go missing all the time," Harrison added. "That's nothing suspicious, Dex. It's their nature. They roam from place to place. These three may have just moved on to another shelter."

"Not to any that I've found," Dex said. "And now a PI breaks into this one and tries to kill another homeless man. Don't you think that warrants an investigation?"

Harrison sighed. "Do you have any evidence suggesting all this is related?"

"Or is this just your imagination looking for problems that aren't there?" Lucas asked.

Anger seized Dex. Granted, he'd been the hothead of the bunch, and had seen his own share of trouble. But sometimes his instincts had been right.

Like it or not, he had to follow his gut.

And that gut told him something was wrong.

MELISSA RUBBED HER hand over her bleary eyes as she sipped her morning coffee. Nightmares of the break-in and shooting had plagued her all night. The feel of the gun against her head…the blood spattering…Smith's shocked face as he stared at her afterward, pain and regret and worry in his expression.

When she'd finally drifted back to sleep, she'd woken up an hour later because she'd thought she'd heard a sound outside. She'd imagined someone breaking into her house. This time she'd been shot and was dying.

A wariness spread over her like a gloomy fog. She was going to turn thirty this year. She was too young to die, especially alone.

Maybe she did want more than work and saving others. Maybe she wanted to carve out a little bit of a life for herself. She'd just been afraid of getting hurt again the way she had with Dex.

She finished her coffee and poured another cup, then phoned April. April offered to contact the volunteers about the center being closed.

"I'll call the detective and see if he'll release the shelter for us to go in and clean up today," Melissa promised. "Then I'll let you know."

She ended the call, then punched the detective's number. The call went straight to voice mail, so she left a message. A knock sounded on her front door just as she finished.

Maybe the detective had come to update her? Or interrogate her again? She hoped it wasn't bad news about Jim Smith, that some overeager cop hadn't gunned him down.

Another knock sounded, and she headed toward the front door to answer it. She checked the peephole, always wary that a stranger might come knocking thinking she was the drug dealer they were searching for. There were at least two on the street that she was aware of.

Her breath caught. Not the detective or a stranger. Dex.

For a moment, she drank in the sight of his handsome face. He wore his cowboy hat, jeans and boots, and the brooding expression that made him look even more mysterious and sexy.

She took a deep breath and opened the door, her heart stuttering as their gazes locked.

"You didn't sleep, did you?" he asked in a gruff voice.

Awareness of his sexuality jolted her nerves. He'd always been intuitive and been able to read her. Maybe that was the reason he'd walked away. He'd sensed she was getting too close, starting to imagine a lifetime with him.

"Not much," she admitted as she motioned for him to come in.

"I'm sorry." He stopped in front of her, his breath huffing out. His six-two frame towered over her. He had big broad shoulders and muscles that had probably made every woman's mouth water when they met him.

She didn't want to think about how many there'd been.

"It's not your fault," she said softly. "But I couldn't stop thinking about Jim and if he was okay. That detective talked like they'd shoot first, then ask questions later."

"You really thought he was a good guy?"

Melissa bit her lip. "Yes. Sure he had secrets. But not everyone who does has a criminal past. Some have just suffered life, and are trying to manage the best they can."

"Like my father," he said, a trace of bitterness to his voice.

Sympathy filled her. "I don't know, Dex. I'm really sorry you didn't have a chance to talk to him and sort things out."

"Me, too." He closed his eyes for a moment, and she realized he was still wrestling with pain and guilt.

She wanted to comfort him. But she clenched her hands by her sides instead. She'd run him off once by becoming too emotional.

She wouldn't do it again.

DEXTER PROMISED HIMSELF he wouldn't make this visit about him and his father, but Melissa had a way of getting to the heart of the matter.

And into his heart.

Focus, man.

"I should have stayed last night," he said.

Melissa shook her head. "Don't be silly, Dex. I'm fine. Now why did you come? Did you hear something from the detective?"

Dexter shook his head. "Afraid not. I'm on my way to McTruitt's office to see if someone there can explain why he was hunting Smith."

"You're investigating this for Detective Lamar?"

"No, but I like mysteries." Or rather, he couldn't let them go until they were solved. He'd always been that way. Always would.

He removed a card from his pocket and offered it to her. "I wanted you to have my number in case you needed something."

Melissa took the card, their hands brushing. She immediately jerked back as if she felt the same tingle he had.

Then she lifted her chin and reached for her purse. "I'm going with you."

"You don't need to do that."

She pressed her hand to his arm. "Yes, I do. I want answers, too, Dex. I can't get into the shelter right now anyway, and I'm going crazy sitting around."

He conceded with a brief nod. No use arguing with Melissa. She might be tenderhearted, but she was also stubborn as hell.

Loud, arguing angry voices from a neighbor drifted their way as they walked to his SUV. Dammit, he didn't like this street or Melissa living here alone.

They rode in silence to McTruitt's office, a faded brick structure in a strip center outside of Austin. Except for a tattoo shop and fertilizer store, the other spaces were deserted, the exteriors run-down.

He parked in front of the building, scanning the property. A black sedan sat in the back parking lot. No one inside. It was too early for the tattoo parlor and the fertilizer store to be open.

A light glowed through the window, indicating that someone was inside. Maybe a secretary? Or McTruitt could have a partner? Damn. He should have done some research on him the night before.

But thoughts of wanting Melissa had distracted him.

He reached for the door to get out. "Wait in the car."

"No, maybe I can help." The silence thickened as they walked up to the building. The door was closed, but Dex saw a flashlight beam moving in the back.

Not a secretary. A man was tossing the place.

He pushed his hand in front of Melissa and murmured for her to go back to the car. But before he could, a bullet shattered the front window and sailed past his head.

Melissa screamed and ducked. He pulled his gun and shouted for her to get down.

Chapter Five

Melissa ducked to the side of the window, glass spraying as it shattered.

"Stay down!" Dex shouted.

She pressed herself against the front wall, her chest heaving as she tried to catch her breath. Dex pulled a gun from his back pocket and fired through the hole in the window.

Inside, footsteps pounded and noises echoed as if someone was turning over furniture. Dex motioned for her to stay where she was, and he inched closer to the window and looked inside. Banging, then a man's voice, and another bullet whizzed by Dex's head.

Melissa screamed as he ducked to avoid being hit. He covered her head with his arms to shield her as another bullet flew past and more glass rained down on the front stoop.

She clung to Dex, the two of them hovering low until a few seconds later, the sound of an engine rent the air. The black sedan in the back parking lot shot around the side of the building, roared past, then flew onto the street.

Dex jumped up and gave chase, firing at the car's

tires, but the vehicle screeched forward and disappeared.

Melissa stood on shaky legs as Dex ran back to her.
"Are you all right?" he asked breathlessly.

She nodded, the realization that she'd been involved
in two shootings in two days sending shock waves
through her. "Are you?"

"Yeah." He removed his Stetson, scrubbed a hand
through his shaggy hair, then set the hat back on his
head with a grunt. "I couldn't get the license plate."

"What's going on?" Melissa asked, trying to piece
together what had happened.

"I don't know, but I'm damn well going to find out."
He wiggled the doorknob on the front door, and the
door squeaked open.

As soon as they entered, Melissa could see that the
office had been ransacked. The space consisted of a
small entryway with a desk and a door leading to the
back. Through the doors, they found the main office, a
large space with an oversize metal desk, filing cabinet
and rolling desk chair. The filing cabinet drawers stood
open, papers were scattered all over the desk and floor
as if files had just been dumped, and the space on the
desk where a computer should have been was empty.

"Either he had his laptop with him or someone took
it," Dex mumbled.

Melissa scanned the disheveled room. "What do you
think they were looking for?"

Dex shrugged. "Who knows? Something to do with
one of his investigations."

"You think it was the person who hired him to find
Jim Smith?"

"That's possible. With McTruitt dead at Smith's

hands, whoever that was might not want his name to come out."

"Or his motive," Melissa said. "Do you think McTruitt was sent to kill Jim?"

Dex's dark gaze met hers. "Maybe. If he had a file on Smith here, that would help." Dex walked over to the desk, pulled on a pair of gloves and started rummaging through the scattered papers.

Melissa shifted, but stooped down on the floor to help search. He tossed her a pair of latex gloves, and she yanked them on. The fact that the person shooting at them might have already found that information and taken it was a real possibility.

But maybe they'd interrupted the intruder before he'd found it, and she and Dex would turn up something helpful.

DEX GRITTED HIS TEETH. He should call Lamar, but first he wanted to look around. He scoured through the papers on the desk, searching for any signs of suspicious activity, specifically anything with Jim Smith's name on it or notes referencing the reason McTruitt was looking for Smith—and why he'd held Melissa at gunpoint to get to him.

According to Melissa, Smith hadn't pulled a gun on McTruitt. It was the other way around, which meant that McTruitt either thought Smith was dangerous, or whoever had hired McTruitt to find Smith wanted him badly enough to tell him to use force.

Or…what if he'd been hired to kill Smith?

Ordering a hit would mean someone had motive.

There were pages of notes on old jobs, mostly cheating spouses, a couple of runaway teens, a case of a stolen dog, and other miscellaneous cases, nothing big or criminal.

"Do you see anything?" Melissa asked.

"Nothing on Smith. You?"

She shook her head and stood, then walked over to the wall and studied a photograph of McTruitt with a group of fishing buddies. Dex glanced at it, then strode to the filing cabinet and shuffled through the files.

The man may have had a computer, but he kept files alphabetized old-school style, with scribbled handwritten notes inside. Again, nothing on Smith.

On a whim, he checked the H section, hoping that the man had information on his father, but no file for Hawk. He started to close the file cabinet drawer, but a business card was stuck in the edge, so he yanked it out.

It was a card for a cattle auction site run by a rancher named Vance Baxter. Dex frowned. He'd heard of Baxter. The man's business was booming. He worked with an expert breeder to raise prize studs.

He wondered why McTruitt had the card in his file, but didn't see how it related to Smith or his own father. Still, he jammed it in his pocket.

Time to call Lamar and tell him about the shooting.

"We'd better step outside." Dex took Melissa's arm. "I have to report this to the police. I don't want him to know we were snooping around in here."

Melissa nodded. "You and Detective Lamar are friends?"

Dex shrugged. "He took me under his wing a few years ago. Since then, he's thrown a few cases my way when he hit a dead end and manpower on the force was spread thin."

Melissa frowned.

"You don't like him, do you?" Dex asked.

Melissa shrugged. "I guess I'm not as trusting of cops as some."

He narrowed his eyes. "Bad experience from the shelter?"

"And growing up." A haunted look passed through her eyes, but she clammed up. Dex wanted to ask more, but Lamar answered the call.

"I came out to McTruitt's office," Dex said. "Someone was here and ransacked the place, and they shot at me and Melissa."

Lamar exploded with a string of expletives. "I'll be right there. And for God's sake, don't touch anything, Dex."

Dex bit back a smile. "Of course not, Lamar. We're waiting outside."

Melissa was watching him with avid curiosity when he hung up. "You don't trust him?"

"I didn't say that," Dex said. "But I'm not going to be shut out of this case. If the attack on Smith has anything to do with the other missing transients, I intend to find out."

A FEW MINUTES LATER, Melissa stood with Dex on the steps to the building as the detective stalked toward them. Anger slashed his craggy features as his gaze traveled from Dex to her.

She forced herself to remain expressionless. She'd learned not to show fear or to react to the men who came to the shelter or she couldn't be effective, and she refused to let this man intimidate her.

"What the hell are you doing here?" Detective Lamar growled.

Dex planted his feet apart in a wide stance, his arms crossed. He looked intimidating himself. "You know why. I want answers about my father—"

"Your father drank himself into a car accident," the detective said with a note of sympathy to his voice. "Why would you think his death is connected to this Smith man or McTruitt?"

A muscle ticked in Dex's jaw. "I don't know. Maybe it's not. But it seems odd to me that I found a card for a shelter in Dad's truck, then other transients have gone missing, and now this shooting at another shelter." Dex narrowed his eyes. "Something is going on, Lamar. You have to admit that."

The detective rubbed a hand down his chin and sighed. "What I think, Dex, is that you still haven't gotten over the fact that your father left, and that you're trying to make something where there isn't anything."

Dex shrugged. "Maybe so. But you know I'm like a dog with a bone. I don't quit until I get answers."

"Then trust me to do my job. If I find out anything related to your father or that these incidents are connected, I'll bring you in."

Dex shifted, his jaw tightening. Detective Lamar angled his head toward Melissa. "And you. What are you doing here?"

Melissa forced her voice to remain steady. "I want to know why this PI wanted Jim bad enough to put a gun to my head."

"She has a point," Dex interjected.

The detective heaved a breath. "I'm looking into that, but what I don't need is two civilians interfering."

He gestured to Dex. "Your friend was almost shot last night, and now you come here and are shot at again. This is dangerous, Dex. Take Ms. Gentry home and keep her out of this so she'll be safe."

Melissa curled her fingers into her palms and dug her nails into them, a trick she'd learned to control her reaction in confrontational situations. "I asked to come with him," she said firmly. "Now why don't you try to find out who shot at us?"

The detective's brows shot up. "I plan to do that, Ms. Gentry. But it would make my job easier if I'm not distracted by worrying about the two of you."

Melissa started to retaliate with a retort, but Dex took her arm. "He's right, Melissa. Why don't you wait in the car?"

Melissa bit her tongue. She didn't like taking orders from either man.

She'd been taking care of herself all her life. She couldn't stop now.

DEX COULD HANDLE a reprimand, but not in front of someone else, especially a woman he cared about.

Cared about?

Why had he thought that? He'd known Melissa a long time ago, but there was nothing between them now. Except his protective instincts kicked in full force when she was around. And he sure as hell didn't want to be shut out of this investigation.

He and Melissa both wanted answers. Answers that he would find.

He brushed her back with his hand. "Melissa, please…?"

For a brief second she looked as if she was going to

argue, but then she glanced back at Lamar, and nodded. He clenched his jaw as he watched her climb into his SUV.

Lamar was texting on his phone when Dex turned back to him.

"Tell me exactly what happened?" Lamar asked.

"Like I said on the phone, someone was inside when we arrived." He gestured toward the parking lot. "I spotted a black sedan in the back."

"Any other vehicles around?"

Dex shook his head. "No. The place was dark inside, except for a flashlight beam. That's how I knew someone was in there."

Lamar studied him. "Then what?"

"I looked in the window to see who it was, but then someone started shooting." He walked over to the window and pointed out the broken glass. "Melissa and I ducked to avoid being hit, then I saw movement inside."

"Was there one person or two?" Lamar asked.

Dex chewed the inside of his cheek. "One. At least I didn't see anyone else."

"How about the car? Anyone inside it when you got here?"

Dex shook his head again. "No. It was empty."

Lamar scribbled something in his pocket notepad. "Did you see what the shooter looked like?"

"Afraid not. Like I said, it was dark inside. And he ran out the back."

"License plate on the car?"

"No." Dex felt like a failure as an investigator. Dammit, he wished he could offer more concrete information. But he'd been too busy dodging bullets and worrying about protecting Melissa to chase the bastard.

Lamar examined the window and peered through the broken glass. He dug a bullet casing from the window edge. "You said he shot at you. Did you fire back?"

Dex didn't want to answer, but he had to. Lamar's people would find two different types of bullets when they searched inside.

"Dex?"

"Yeah." He removed his weapon from the back of his jeans and held it out to Lamar. "I fired twice. You can check."

Lamar's gaze met his. "Did you hit him?"

"I don't think so. I was just trying to warn him off."

Lamar scoffed. "You know I could haul you in."

"But you aren't going to," Dex said. "Because technically I fired in self-defense. And you, my friend, don't want to waste time when it'll go nowhere."

Besides, he hadn't really crossed the line.

He would, though, if necessary, to find out the truth about Smith and what was going on with these shelters.

MELISSA WATCHED THE interchange between Dex and Detective Lamar, her curiosity piqued as to how the two of them had met and become friends.

Her phone buzzed, and she checked the number, expecting it to be her coworker April. Instead the name of the director at another shelter appeared. Candace Fuller from Retreat. She'd once worked closely with Candace and they still had coffee on occasion.

She quickly connected the call.

"Melissa, I heard about the shooting. Are you all right?"

"I'm fine," Melissa said, then explained what had

happened. "The police are looking for Smith, but I don't think he's dangerous. He saved my life."

"I'm just glad you're okay." Candace paused. "There's another reason I called."

Melissa tapped her fingers on her leg. She didn't like the worry in her friend's voice. "What's wrong?"

"A man named Bill Small at Retreat thinks something has happened to one of his friends. He claims he disappeared."

"Did you report it to the police?" Melissa asked.

Candace sighed. "Yes, but they don't seem concerned."

Sounded typical. A crime scene van pulled into the parking lot, and she saw Dex heading toward her.

"Why does Bill think something happened to his friend?" Melissa asked.

"He saw the story about some other missing homeless men, and said his friend expressed concern over them, too. He disappeared the next day."

Melissa's breath stalled in her chest. "Is Bill still at Retreat?"

"Yes."

"I'm with a private detective right now, Candace. We'll stop by and talk to Bill."

Chapter Six

Thirty minutes later, Dex parked at Retreat, his curiosity aroused by what Melissa had told him. Lamar's last words echoed in his head.

"Let me do the police work. And leave Melissa out of it or you're going to get her killed."

His friend had always cautioned him about overstepping, but today his warning had sounded different. Almost like a threat. As if he didn't stay out of it, Lamar would see that his PI license might be revoked? That he'd lock him up for interfering?

He didn't give a damn. No one stopped Dexter Hawk when he was on a mission.

"Tell me about this shelter," Dex said as they walked up to the entryway.

"Because of its location, it's one of the busiest," Melissa said. "I worked with Candace for a short while until a position opened up at Lend-A-Hand."

'Why did you make the move?"

Melissa shrugged. "I just saw a need," she said quietly, but didn't elaborate, making him wonder if it was one of the shelters she'd lived in as a child. Her father had dragged her around Texas, dumping them wherever and whenever he pleased.

"They house close to a hundred people here at any time," she said. "We work with the court system and advocates for domestic violence and abuse to find places when needed for women and children, but there are a lot of men in need, too. This one stays pretty full most of the time." She hesitated at the door and pressed the intercom buzzer for entry.

Dex swallowed hard as he scanned the property. It was set off from the street in a wooded section that shielded the cement block building from passersby on the road and was surrounded by a tall metal fence. For the residents' protection or for the people who lived nearby in the housing projects that had been built a half mile from the shelter? Probably both.

The volunteer buzzed them in, and Melissa led the way. A young blonde about Melissa's age greeted them and hugged Melissa, murmuring concern about the shooting the day before.

"Candace, this is Dexter Hawk," Melissa said as the women pulled apart. "He's a private investigator and a friend."

Candace gave him an assessing look. "Hawk, that name sounds familiar."

Dex offered her a smile. "My family owns a ranch in Tumbleweed. You may have read about my brother Lucas, who shut down a human trafficking ring recently."

"That's right," Candace said. "And your other brother is a lawyer."

"There are four of us," Dex said. "My oldest brother, Harrison, is sheriff of Tumbleweed."

Melissa cleared her throat. "Dex is looking into the man who saved my life yesterday. He's also been inves-

tigating the disappearance of a couple of other homeless men who've gone missing."

"You suspect foul play?" Candace asked.

Dex shrugged. "It's too early to tell. But if someone is preying on these men, I want to find out who
and why."

"Can we talk to Bill now?" Melissa asked.

"Of course." Candace led the way through a small
entry into a large dining area where men sat finishing
breakfast and drinking coffee.

She and Melissa stopped to chat with several of them,
and Dex spoke to a few men, although they looked wary
of him and didn't have much to say. Maybe they thought
he was law enforcement although he was dressed in
jeans and his cowboy hat.

Seeing so many needy men made him wonder if he
should talk to his brothers about hiring a couple as ranch
hands. Something to check into. Although the safety
of his family and the foster girls took priority. Still, if
they grew the cattle side of the business, they'd need
more hands.

Candace paused at a long table near the door to the
kitchen where an old-timer in grimy overalls sat alone.
She and Melissa exchanged looks of concern as Candace stood by the table. The young woman laid her
hand on the man's shoulder and leaned over to speak
to him.

He gave a little nod, then looked up at Melissa. A
tentative smile softened the harsh age lines bracket-
ing his mouth, which tightened when he spotted Dex.

"It's okay," Candace said softly as she introduced
him as Bill Small. "Melissa and Dex are here to help

find out what happened to your friend. I need you to tell them your story."

Bill glanced into his cup of coffee as if it would give him answers, then pushed out the chair beside him, inviting Melissa to sit down. Dex walked to the opposite side of the table and claimed a chair across from Bill, then accepted a cup of coffee from Candace.

"You a cop?" Bill asked with a wary look.

Dex shook his head. "A PI. My father lived in a shelter and recently died. That started me looking at the shelters for answers about him, then I learned that several men had gone missing."

Bill's expression softened. "Sorry about your daddy."

Dex nodded. He couldn't escape the grief. "Me, too. And I'm sorry about your friend."

The simple exchange calmed Bill. He took a sip of his coffee, wiped his mouth on a paper napkin, then set the cup down. "His name was Harry Willis. I think something bad happened to him."

"What makes you think that?" Melissa asked.

Bill drummed crooked fingers on the table as if trying to put together his words. "Harry was kind of a loner, about my age," Bill said. "But he had a daughter."

"Did he keep in touch with her?" Dex asked.

Bill shook his head. "Not really. But he recently learned she had a baby. He wanted to see that kid more than anything. He was saving up money to send to his girl, hoping she'd let him visit."

Melissa murmured a sympathetic sound. "Did he go see her?"

Bill raked a hand through his thinning white hair.

"Naw, at least I don't think so. But one night he showed up here with a wad of cash."

Dex frowned. "Did he say where he got the money?"

"Said he did a favor for someone, and they paid him. But that worried me. He wouldn't say who it was or what he did."

"Could it have been a drug deal?" Melissa asked.

Bill shook his head. "Harry didn't do drugs, and would never have sold 'em."

Money was a powerful motivator. "Not even for money to send his daughter?" Dex asked.

"No way," Bill said firmly. "His son OD'd when he was only nineteen. That's what drove Harry to the streets. The guilt."

Dex understood about guilt.

"So what happened after you talked to him about the money?" Melissa asked.

"Next day he said he was going to mail it to his daughter. Left to walk to the post office but never came back."

Silence, thick with tension, stretched between them for a full minute. "Maybe he decided to take it to his daughter in person instead of mailing it," Dex suggested.

Melissa's gaze met his. "Or someone could have stolen it from him."

The implication that he'd been killed for the money rang between them, but neither voiced it aloud.

Dex mentally made a plan. First, he'd check with the daughter to see if she'd heard from her father.

If she hadn't, he'd check police reports and the morgue in case Harry had shown up in jail...or dead.

MELISSA HATED THE thoughts running through her head, that Harry might be dead. The men who needed their help moved around constantly. She and her father certainly had. Sure, they became friendly with others staying at the shelter, but usually not for long.

The center's goal was to help them rejoin the work force, and take charge of their lives. They facilitated family reconciliations through counseling, assisted in arranging financial assistance, and offered programs to aid in mainstreaming the men back into society.

If someone moved of their own accord, it was usually because they didn't form attachments or weren't ready to accept the help offered. Pride, depression, mental illness, addictions, physical injuries or illness, emotional trauma, past criminal activities, imprisonment and PTSD were contributing factors that landed the men on the streets and were obstacles to recovery.

"Did he have any friends that he might go to or turn to for help?" Melissa asked.

Bill scratched his chin. "Said he never stayed anywhere long enough to make friends. Got antsy if he was in one place too long. He used to work odd jobs on ranches across the state when he was younger. But arthritis kicked in and joints hurt too bad for physical labor."

Melissa gestured around the room to the other men who were dispersing. "Did you ask to see if anyone knew the nature of the job Harry did?"

"Sure did. Ms. Candace talked to them, too. But no one knew anything about the money or where it came from."

"You said he liked to move around," Dex cut in.

"Other than the money, what makes you think he didn't panic about seeing his daughter and move on to another city?"

Bill pushed away from the table and stood, then picked up his coffee. "Come on, I'll show you."

Melissa and Dex followed Bill as he carried his cup to the counter and left it to be washed. In the bunk rooms, he went to the back wall and the bed at the end.

Bill squatted down and pulled an old duffel bag from beneath the bed, then set it on the cot. "This was all Harry had to his name." His sad eyes met Melissa's, then he removed a photograph and showed it to them. "This was the only picture he had of his daughter. Was taken when she was five. Harry never would have left without it."

Melissa's heart squeezed. Bill was right. Most people kept a memento of their past life that they clung to and carried with them wherever they went. Her father had held on to a pocket watch that had belonged to his own father. She'd kept a picture of her mother that her father knew nothing about. It was in her wallet now.

"There's something else." Bill carefully placed the picture back in the bag.

"What?" Melissa asked.

"The day he left, I saw someone watching him. A car, a black sedan, was parked down the street. When Harry started toward the post office, it pulled out and drove real slow behind him."

Melissa's gaze locked with Dex's. The man who'd shot at them at McTruitt's office had been driving a black sedan.

DEX'S SUSPICIONS KICKED up a notch at the idea of the same black sedan following Harry as the one at Mc-Truitt's office. It was possible it was a different car, but everything Bill said made him wonder if Bill was right to suspect his friend had fallen prey to foul play.

He gestured toward the duffel. "Do you mind if I look through that bag?"

Bill glanced at Melissa, who nodded that it was okay, and Bill moved aside to give Dex access. He handed Bill the photo. "Hold on to that. I wouldn't want it to get damaged."

Bill's look of gratitude warmed Dex's heart. He'd just won the man's trust and respect. Bill ran his finger over the picture with a sad smile as Dex searched the bag. The larger section held assorted clothing. One outer pocket contained chewing gum, a fast-food wrapper from a burger joint and an empty water bottle. A small section in front held a few toiletries. He dug deeper into the inner pocket and discovered a slip of paper with a name on it.

Sally Layton.

"Was Sally the daughter's name?" he asked Bill.

Bill nodded. "Yeah."

A business card was tucked inside the folded scrap of paper. Dex flipped it over and saw it was a card for a large animal vet.

Dr. Bart Huckleberry. He specialized in large animal medicine and worked closely with an expert cattle breeder.

Why would Harry have a card for the vet in his pocket?

He tapped it on his hand. "Did Harry mention anything about a vet to you?"

Bill shook his head. "No, why?"

"I found this card in his bag. Maybe the vet is connected to the job he did."

Bill shrugged as if he had no idea.

"I'll talk to him." Dex tucked the clothing back in the bag, but stuffed the business card in his pocket.

Sympathy tinged Melissa's expression, and she patted Bill on the back. "Let us know if you hear anything from Harry. And we'll do the same."

Bill cradled Melissa's hand between his. "Thank you so much for listening to me and trying to help."

Melissa gave the older man a hug. "Of course."

Admiration for Melissa and her role in helping these homeless men mushroomed in Dex's chest.

Bill extended his hand, and Dex shook it. "Thank you, too, Mr. Dex."

Dex cleared his throat. "We'll do everything we can to find your friend." He just hoped they found Harry, and that when they did, he was still alive.

Chapter Seven

As he drove away from the shelter, Dexter couldn't shake the feeling that Bill's friend might be dead. Needing to verify the facts, he veered into the parking lot of a place called the Barbecue Pit.

"Let's get a late lunch," he said as he snagged his phone. "I want to see if I can locate Harry's daughter before we visit the vet."

"I could eat," Melissa said softly, reminding him that she loved burgers and barbecue and wasn't one of those picky women who only ate rabbit food.

The popular café boasted the best brisket in Austin, and was decorated Western-style, with a metal pig beneath a rustic wagon wheel, surrounded by beef cattle made from metal and wire.

"I know learning about your sister and your father was difficult," Melissa said as they settled at a booth in the corner. "How's your family doing?"

Dex pushed the menu aside. He knew what he wanted.

Time with Melissa.

Dammit, he couldn't have that. He had to focus.

"Everyone's hanging in there," he said gruffly.

The waitress appeared, and he paused so they could

order. Melissa asked for a pulled pork sandwich and iced tea while he ordered the pork plate and coffee.

"Of course we were hoping to find Chrissy and Dad alive, but after eighteen years, I guess we'd all prepared ourselves for the fact that might not happen. The sad thing is that Chrissy's death was really accidental. The guy who killed her was mentally challenged and infatuated with kids. He just wanted to play with her, and got too rough when she tried to leave." The waitress brought their drinks, and he sipped his coffee. "Unfortunately, the guy's mother covered for him to protect him. That was a mistake."

"He did the same thing to some other children, didn't he?" Melissa asked.

Dex nodded, the guilt back.

Melissa covered his hand with hers. A tingle of warmth shot through him, making him shift in his seat. He'd always liked Melissa's touch. Her hands were so gentle. Soft. Filled with tenderness and love.

A love he didn't deserve. Chrissy wouldn't have died if he'd watched her that night.

"I realize you blamed yourself," Melissa said in that uncanny way she'd always had of reading him. Maybe that was the reason he'd left her. He didn't like anyone seeing his vulnerabilities.

"But I hope you've let that go, Dex. You were all just kids. Siblings argue and fight. Your sister obviously adored all of you, or else she wouldn't have followed along. That night was just a series of unfortunate events." She squeezed his hand, and he had to force himself not to turn his palm over and clasp hands as if they were a couple. "Like you said, it was an accident," she said softly. "Your sister wouldn't have wanted you to blame yourself."

She was right. On an intellectual level he knew that. But his heart and conscience refused to let him off the hook.

MELISSA SENSED DEX was still beating himself up over his little sister's death as they dug into their food. She wished she knew how to help him move past it.

She wiped barbecue sauce from her mouth. "Your mother took in some of the victims of that human trafficking ring, didn't she?"

Dex nodded and shoveled up a forkful of coleslaw. "Yeah, it's been great for everyone. Mom struggled after Chrissy disappeared. Then when Dad left, I think she blamed herself because he abandoned us. The house was quiet, sad, for a long time."

"Even with four boys in it?" Melissa asked.

Dex chuckled. "Well, maybe it wasn't always quiet. But my brothers and I bore the brunt of guilt over the whole thing. We kind of all shut down for a while, retreated into ourselves, tried not to make trouble and upset her even more."

Melissa gave him a sympathetic look. "You mean *you* behaved?"

Dex chuckled. "For a little while. But then I couldn't help myself. I was angry and took it out on everyone. I started breaking all the rules."

Dex's mischievous, daredevil attitude had drawn her from the beginning. He was a bad boy, yet he had morals and fought for the underdog. A potent combination. Ignoring the seed of desire sprouting inside her, she finished her meal while he excused himself to make a phone call to his brother Lucas. Maybe his brother could locate Harry's daughter and she could tell them if he was all right.

"HER NAME IS Sally Layton," Dex told Lucas. "She's the daughter of a homeless man who might be missing."

"Hang on, I'll see what I can find."

Dex paced by the men's room as he waited. Dammit, he needed distance from Melissa. Talking to her, being with her again, stirred old feelings that he thought he'd left behind in the dust.

"I found her," Lucas said as he came back on the line. "She's a nurse at a clinic near the main hospital. I'll text you her address and phone number."

Dex thanked him and hung up, then waited on the text. When the address appeared on his screen, he called the clinic but Sally wasn't at work. He returned to the table and paid the bill, then he and Melissa drove to the woman's house.

Sally lived in a neighborhood with small ranch homes that appeared to have been updated.

"These are nice," Melissa said.

"They remind me of the homes Harrison's wife, Honey, renovates. She bought a bunch of older places in Lower Tumbleweed and has completely revived the town." Melissa should be living in a cute little house like this, not in that dump where she was now.

A station wagon sat in the driveway, and a flower bed filled with impatiens in various colors brightened the neatly kept yard. The front porch boasted two rocking chairs, making the place look homey and inviting.

They walked up to the house in silence, and Dex knocked. Footsteps, then a voice sounded inside. A few seconds later, the door opened. A petite blonde carrying a baby stood at the door, rocking the infant in her arms.

Melissa's expression softened as she looked at the infant, a hint of yearning in her eyes. Dex shifted, wondering why she'd never married and had a family herself. Although the thought of her with another man didn't sit well in his gut.

"Sally?" Melissa said.

The young woman nodded and glanced between the two of them. "Can I help you?"

Dex gestured for Melissa to take the lead, and she explained about their visit with Bill.

Sally's eyes widened. "You've seen my father?"

"I'm afraid not," Melissa said softly. "I work at a homeless shelter called Lend-A-Hand. Earlier, we spoke with a man named Bill at another shelter."

Pain wrenched the young woman's face. "My father is in a homeless shelter?"

"He was," Melissa said.

"His friend Bill is worried because Harry left and hasn't come back. Have you seen or talked to him recently?" Dex asked.

The baby started fussing, and Sally lifted the child and patted its back, soothing it. "Not in months. I kept hoping he'd contact me." She pressed a kiss to the infant's head. "Sari is two months old today. I wanted Dad to meet his granddaughter."

Melissa smiled. "Bill said that Harry had just earned

some cash and that he was going to send it to you. He wanted to see you and the baby."

A sliver of hope sparkled in the woman's eyes, but worry quickly replaced it. Or maybe it was disappointment. Dex knew what it was like to wonder where your father was and why he'd left.

"But I haven't heard from him." Her voice cracked. "He probably just changed his mind. It wouldn't be the first time."

A heartbeat passed, then Melissa squeezed Sally's hand. "Did you know he carries a picture of you wherever he goes?"

Tears moistened Sally's eyes, but she blinked them away and shook her head.

"Dad blamed himself for my brother's death, but it wasn't Dad's fault. I tried to reconnect with him, but Dad started drinking and disappeared."

"I'm so sorry," Melissa said softly.

Dex removed a business card from his pocket and offered it to her. "Please call me if you hear from him."

Sadness tinged Sally's expression. "If you find him, please tell him that I love him, and that I want him to come home."

Compassion filled Dex, and he nodded, his throat too thick to speak.

Melissa reached out and stroked the baby's head. "She's beautiful."

"Thanks," Sally whispered. "I just hope Dad gets to meet her." A tear trickled down Sally's cheek and Melissa hugged the young woman.

"I hope so, too," Melissa said. "We'll keep in touch."

Sally hugged the baby tighter and closed the door.

Melissa wiped a tear from her cheek as they walked back to the car, and they settled inside in silence.

He hoped to hell Sally's search had a better ending than his had.

MELISSA TWISTED HER hands together, her nerves on edge as they drove toward the vet's office. So many sad stories of families torn apart. Tragic circumstances, folks wandering around homeless and alone while the people they left behind struggled with grief and fear and guilt. She wished she could give them all a happy ending, but she'd learned a long time ago that she couldn't. She'd expected to become immune to the pain, but each story got to her.

Dex's face looked strained as he drove. No doubt he was probably thinking about his own father and how he and his family had wanted him to return. They'd waited eighteen years only to find him dead in a DUI accident. That had to be a hard blow.

Dex veered off the main road down a bumpy country one with acres of farmland spread out on both sides. A rustic wooden sign bearing the name Huckleberry Animal Hospital dangled from a post as Dex steered the SUV toward the clinic.

It was situated about thirty miles outside of Austin on farmland equipped with emergency facilities, as well as barns and stables for livestock if the animals needed housing for treatment. A mobile unit and attached trailer used to travel to farms and ranches was parked by the main office.

"Do you think Harry is dead?" Melissa finally asked, breaking the strained silence as they bounced over the ruts in the road.

"I don't know," Dex said. "The bodies of the three men recently reported missing haven't been found, so they may still be alive. Lamar could be right, and I'm looking for trouble and connections when there is none."

"But you may be onto something," Melissa said. "We have to find out, Dex."

"I won't argue with that." His mouth twitched. "Can I ask you something?"

Melissa tensed. She refused to admit he'd broken her heart. Maybe he'd walked away and hadn't given her a second thought. She didn't want to know if that was the case. It hurt too much to think the feelings she'd imagined between them had been completely one-sided. "Depends on what it is."

"Fair enough." He parked by the mobile unit and cut the engine. "Did you and your father stay at Retreat when you were young?"

Melissa averted her gaze, afraid he'd see too much. There was agony in her heart when she remembered roaming from one place to another, sleeping in the car, or a park, or an alley. And the shame.

She'd always been so ashamed.

"No," she said honestly. "It's reserved for single men."

He nodded in understanding. "How about Candace? Did you two meet through work?"

"Yes and no. We met in college when we were both volunteering at a women's shelter. We instantly bonded over shared goals." She rubbed her finger over a silver charm on a chain around her neck. "We've been close friends ever since, although she married last year, so we haven't seen each other quite as much lately."

"Doesn't her husband worry about her working at a men's shelter?"

Melissa laughed softly. "Yes, but he loves her, and he knows that her work is a part of her, that she's passionate about it. I think it's one reason he fell in love with her. How could he ask her to give it up?"

Dex's dark eyes flickered with some emotion she couldn't define. "You're right. He couldn't."

A second later, he opened his car door and slid out. Melissa joined him, and they walked side by side up to the vet's office, a long building that looked as if it was once a barn that had been converted. A tin roof topped the dark red painted building. Dex was scanning the property as if anticipating trouble, and she did the same.

In the distance, she spotted two horses galloping across a field, but no cattle. A small herd of goats roamed the field to the right, and a gray cat lay sleeping on the front porch of the brick ranch house. The driveway to the house was empty.

The area seemed unusually quiet, as if no one was around. Maybe Dr. Huckleberry was on a call.

Except his mobile unit was parked in front.

Perhaps he had a second one or only took the mobile unit when necessary. Routine calls might not require all his medical supplies. Or heck, he could just be running an errand.

Dex knocked, then called out for the doctor as he opened the metal door. "Dr. Huckleberry?"

Silence greeted them as they entered, then the scent of strong cleaning chemicals hit her. The cement floor looked fairly clean, an office with a desk to greet clients facing the door. It was empty. Did Huckleberry have a secretary? An assistant?

Dex strode past the desk through a double door, and Melissa followed, an eerie quiet enveloping her as they checked two exam rooms, a surgical unit and a room that served as the pharmacy. A locked glass case held medical supplies and drugs. Everything appeared to be intact.

They walked through a hallway to find a small office in back. A metal desk and filing cabinet were the only pieces of furniture. The office was empty, as well. A calendar on the wall marked the days, an appointment book lay on the desk and the bottom desk drawer stood slightly ajar.

Dex gave it a quick glance and scanned the desk, but didn't touch anything. A photograph on the wall showcased the vet receiving an award. The man was probably in his midforties, with a stout frame, a thick beard and chunky hands.

Dex gestured toward a back exit leading out to the barn. The sound of a dog barking met them as he opened the door.

A big gray shepherd-mix dog greeted them, its head cocked. Melissa froze, giving the dog time to sniff her and recognize that they didn't pose a threat.

"Shh, buddy, it's all right." Dex leaned over to pet the dog, his hand halting in midair. He muttered a curse, then shot her a look that indicated something was wrong.

Melissa inched closer, and Dex gestured toward the dog's nose. Melissa sucked in a sharp breath. Blood.

Dex rubbed the back of the dog's head. "Show me what happened, buddy." He pulled his gun and motioned for her to stay behind him as they followed the shepherd across the back of the property.

SENSES HONED FOR TROUBLE, Dex gripped his gun at the ready as he hurried behind the shepherd. They passed a small barn, which appeared empty at the moment. The dog barked again, then turned to see if Dex was following.

"I'm right behind you, bud," he said, then picked up his pace as the dog broke into a run.

Melissa raced behind him. Dry brush crunched beneath his boots as he passed a stable and veered toward a second barn. The sound of cows mooing echoed from the building, then another sound that made his pulse jump.

An angry bull stomping, banging and snorting. He held his hand up, warning Melissa to wait while he checked out the situation.

The dog barked at the open door to the barn, pawing at the dirt and turning circles. "You stay here, too," he murmured to the shepherd as he inched inside the building.

Stalls on both sides of the barn flanked a hallway. He eased down the hallway, glancing into each stall in case someone lay in wait. Two cows were housed in separate stalls on the left. The angry bull was on the right at the end. The sight of something dark that looked like blood on the rough wood floor caught his eye, and he stooped to examine it.

Definitely blood.

His senses became more alert. He couldn't afford to be caught off guard and walk into an ambush.

The stamping and snorting grew louder, and the

wooden slats on the stall door vibrated as the angry animal pounded the locked stall door.

Dex had a healthy respect for cattle and horses. He could handle both. But both could be dangerous. A few attempts at bull riding in a local rodeo had taught him the power of the beast.

He approached slowly, and peered over the stall edge. One bull. The angry animal huffed and dug his hooves into the dirt where a man lay, facedown. His clothes were ripped to shreds and drenched in blood.

"Dex?" Melissa called.

"Call 9-1-1," he shouted.

Although judging from the man's slack body and the amount of blood loss, they were too late.

Chapter Eight

Melissa gasped at the sight of the man on the stall floor. "Oh, God... Is that the vet?"

"Yeah, looks like he was gored to death by that bull."

Her mind was reeling as she pulled her phone from her pocket, punched 9-1-1 and backed away from the stall. The operator answered, and she explained what they'd found. "We need an ambulance and the police."

Her back brushed something hard, then someone grabbed her from behind. She shrieked and dropped her phone, then a cold hand clamped over her mouth.

Panic shot through her, and she kicked and clawed at the man's arms.

A bullet suddenly whizzed by her head. It had come from behind her. Then another.

She kicked the man again, then bit down on his hand as hard as she could. He cursed and yanked his hand away for a second, but slammed his fist against the side of her head, and she saw stars.

Dex leaned against the wall to avoid being hit by the bullet. Her captor dragged her toward the door while the shooter fired again. Dex fired back and hit the shooter, who dropped to the floor with a grunt. But a bullet from the second shooter pinged by her head.

The man holding her gripped her tighter and pulled her near the door. Dex fired again, and the man shoved her into the stall. He spun around to fire at Dex, but Melissa jumped him from behind.

He tried to shove her off, but she jabbed at his eyes. More gunfire in the barn. She prayed Dex was all right. Meanwhile she had to fight for her life.

The man tried to pry her hands from his face. She struggled to stay on his back, but he was strong and threw her to the floor. Her head hit the back of the stall, and the world spun. But she spied a cabinet with medical supplies in the corner and scrambled toward it.

The man lunged toward her. She grabbed a hypodermic just before the man reached for her neck.

She gripped the hypodermic and jabbed upward, driving it into his belly as his hands closed around her throat.

He squeezed her neck, choking her. She kicked out and pushed at his arms, determined to free herself, but he dug his meaty paws into her throat again, cutting off the air to her windpipe.

She clawed at him, but his hold tightened and a dizzy spell overcame her. Her vision blurred, then everything went black, and her hands fell limp to her side.

She fought to remain conscious, but the darkness was sucking her in, pulling her into an endless tunnel where she kept falling and spinning. As hard as she tried, she couldn't grab hold of anything to hang on to.

DEX INCHED FORWARD, plastering himself against the barn wall to avoid another bullet. Dammit. One man was down. He thought he'd hit the second, but the bastard hadn't given up.

And where the hell was Melissa? In that stall on the end by the door? Sweat beaded on his skin. He couldn't see her, and he didn't like it.

Another shot. Anger propelled him forward. He aimed his gun at the stall where the shooter had taken refuge, firing bullets through the slats. A grunt echoed from the inside, and he raced to cross the distance, firing another round as he glanced inside.

The man was finally down. Blood soaked his shirt and spattered the wall and floor. He darted inside, grabbed the man's gun, then checked his pulse.

Dead.

Now, he had to get to Melissa.

He loaded another magazine into his weapon, then slowly crept toward her. It was too quiet ahead. Had the man managed to drag Melissa outside?

Fear made him hurry, and he checked left and right, maneuvering closer. A noise echoed from the stall, and he jerked around in front of it, his gun aimed.

The bastard who'd attacked Melissa lay on the floor, unmoving. So did Melissa. She looked pale and limp, a hypodermic on the floor beside her open hand.

Dear God, she had to be all right.

He raced into the stall, quickly dropped down beside the man and checked him for a pulse. Low but thready. He was alive but didn't appear to be stirring.

Keeping one eye on the bastard, he rushed to Melissa, knelt and pressed two fingers to her neck. Precious seconds passed. Finally a pulse.

He muttered another prayer, then gently brushed his hand against her cheek.

"Melissa, come back to me."

Slowly, her chest rose and fell.

Heart hammering, he brushed her cheek again. "Talk to me, darlin'."

A flutter of her eyelids. Her breath quickened, and she emitted a soft gasp.

He slid one hand below her head to raise her to an incline position, murmuring soft words of comfort. Yet the handprints on her neck made him want to curse and kill the man on the floor beside her.

"It's all right, I'm here," he murmured softly.

Her eyelids slowly opened, then closed. She lifted one hand and reached for his arm. He wrapped his arm around her, holding her and rocking her back and forth while she slowly regained consciousness.

A siren wailed outside.

She blinked again, her voice raspy as she whispered his name.

"I'm here, darlin'." He held her close, his chest aching as he waited on the ambulance to arrive.

Melissa could have died today. And yesterday. Who was the bastard on the floor and the dead man in the stall?

They had to be working for someone, but whom?

Someone who knew he and Melissa were asking questions? Someone who didn't want them to find answers...

MELISSA SLOWLY RETURNED to reality. Her head was throbbing from where she'd hit it against the wall, and her throat felt raw.

But she was in Dex's arms, and that felt right.

The last thing she remembered was gasping for air and wondering if Dex had been shot.

She blinked, struggling to clear her vision. Dex's handsome face slowly slipped into view. His strong jaw rough with a constant five o'clock shadow. His dark serious eyes.

"Melissa, that hypodermic? Did he inject you?"

She shook her head. "No, I jabbed it in his chest." She gulped. "Did I kill him?"

Dex shook his head, then glanced at the cabinet of medical supplies. "That was probably a tranquilizer that the vet used." He cupped her face between his hands. "But if you had killed him, it would have been all right. He tried to kill you."

"What about the other shooters?" Melissa asked.

Dex's jaw tightened. "Both dead."

The sound of the siren wailing drew closer. Dex heaved a breath.

Melissa clutched Dex's arm as he helped her stand. Her legs felt weak, and she was trembling, but the fresh air revived her as they stepped from the barn. She clung to him as they made their way across the space between the barn and main clinic, where she sat down on a bench.

A police car raced up and screeched to a stop, gravel spewing. An ambulance roared up on its tail. Detective Lamar unfolded his legs from the front of the police cruiser.

Two medics exited the ambulance and jogged toward them. Dex waved them over to her. The detective scowled at her and then at Dex.

"What the hell is going on with you?" Detective

Lamar growled. "Everywhere you go, bodies are piling up."

Dex muttered an apology. "I drove out to talk to the vet and found him dead. Then three men came out of nowhere and jumped us."

"Where are they now?" Detective Lamar asked.

Dex shifted, removed his Stetson, raked a hand through his hair, then settled his hat back on his head. He had a habit of doing that when he was stalling. "In the barn. Two dead. Melissa fought off the other and managed to inject him with some drug. I think it was probably a tranquilizer."

Dex gestured toward the stall holding the unconscious man.

"Get him first," Detective Lamar ordered. "And I want to talk to him as soon as he regains consciousness." The detective wiped sweat from his brow. "Now I need to see Dr. Huckleberry."

Dex pressed a hand to the detective's chest. "Wait, it's dangerous, Lamar. Let me coach that bull into another stall before you go in."

The medic began to examine Melissa as Dex led the detective and the second medic deeper into the barn.

When the female medic was satisfied that Melissa's breathing was normal and there didn't appear to be permanent damage to her throat, she joined the others to assist with the injured man.

Melissa traced her fingers over the bruising on her neck, grateful she'd survived. A slight wind picked up, stirring the hot summer air, and she coughed as she inhaled dust.

Her eye caught sight of something red sticking out

from the corner of the doorway. She stood and went to see what it was.

She stooped down to pull at it. It was a red bandanna. She tugged it from the splintered wood where it had caught and examined it.

It looked exactly like the bandanna Jim Smith had been carrying.

IT TOOK DEX finessing and time to steer the bull into the neighboring stall so Lamar could examine the vet. While he handled the animal, Lamar examined the two dead shooters.

Dex joined him just as Lamar was digging through the pocket of the first dead man. Blood stained his body, clothes, the wall and floor.

Lamar snapped pictures of the man, the bullet holes and bullet casings in the wall and stall, along with the 9mm weapon still clutched in the dead man's hand, then examined the second man.

"So what do you think happened with the doc?" Lamar asked Dex.

Dex chewed over theories. "These men killed Huckleberry, then put him in the stall with the bull to make it appear accidental." Dex explained about his conversation with Bill regarding Bill's friend Harry as he showed him to Huckleberry's body.

"I think you're grasping at straws trying to connect Huckleberry's death to the missing homeless men. Huckleberry worked with prize bulls and a breeding expert. These men could have planned to steal drugs, or maybe they thought he kept some of the bull's seed here."

That was feasible.

"Did you touch anything?" Lamar asked.

Dex shook his head. "I used work gloves to rope the bull and move him." As much for his own protection as to keep his prints off the place.

The bull was still stomping and butting his head against the wood slats next door. Lamar startled, a dark scowl growing on his face as he photographed the bloody scene, then stepped inside.

"I don't see bullet casings like I found with the other two dead men," Lamar said as he examined the barn walls. "Considering the fact these men were armed, it seems logical that would be their murder weapon of choice."

"So you think I'm wrong?" Dex asked.

"Too soon to say. But it's possible Huckleberry got trapped with the bull and the animal killed him."

Dex didn't believe for a minute that Huckleberry's death was an accident. "What about the shooters?"

Lamar grunted. "Like I said, maybe they were thieves." He scrutinized the stall again. "I suppose one of them could have drugged the vet, then threw him in here with the bull. I'll make sure the ME runs a tox screen."

Drugging Huckleberry and then putting him in the stall made sense. If Dex hadn't shown up, the men might have gotten away with their plan, too.

Lamar crossed the stall, then squatted down beside the vet. The man lay on his side, clothes torn, body mauled. Lamar looked at his chest, then rolled him to his side to examine his back. He was looking for gunshot wounds, cause of death.

"No bullet wounds. He's not in full rigor, either, so he hasn't been dead long."

The female medic appeared behind them. "The medical examiner and crime scene techs are here. We're ready to transport the surviving man to the hospital."

"How is he?" Lamar asked.

"Vitals are stable, but he's still unconscious." She angled her head. "No ID on him. Do you know who he is or if he has family?"

Dex shook his head.

"We'll run both men's prints and DNA." Voices echoed from the front of the barn, then the medical examiner walked toward them, followed by two crime techs.

Dex leaned against the stable door, anxious to learn the identity of Melissa's attacker. When he regained consciousness, maybe he'd talk.

"I'm going to check on Melissa."

Lamar cleared his throat. "You two need to stick around for a few more minutes. I have to take her statement."

Dex nodded and went to see Melissa. She was still sitting on that bench, looking lost and shaken as she watched the ambulance pull away. But when she saw him, she lifted her chin, the fight returning to her eyes.

"You okay?" he asked as he approached her.

"Yeah. Do you know who those men were?"

"Not yet." He noticed the red bandanna in her hands. "Where did that come from?"

An odd look flashed across her face, and she stuffed it in her pocket. "It's nothing."

Dex narrowed his eyes. Why did he sense she was hiding something?

Voices from the barn and then footsteps brought

their conversation to a halt. Lamar strode toward them, talking in a hushed tone to the ME.

"I'll let you know the results of the autopsy as soon as I finish," the ME told Lamar.

Lamar thanked him, then stopped in front of him and Melissa. "Ms. Gentry, I need you to tell me what happened here today."

Melissa looked wary, but explained about Bill's concerns over Harry. "Bill thinks that someone hurt Harry because of some cash Harry had."

"How much are you talking?" Lamar asked.

"He didn't say," Melissa said. "Harry was also secretive about how he earned it. He left for the post office to mail the money to his daughter, but she never received it. Bill thought someone in a black sedan was following Harry when he left the shelter."

"What makes you think that Harry has something to do with Dr. Huckleberry?"

"We found a card with his name on it in Harry's things," Dex said.

Lamar made a low sound in his throat. "Everywhere you two go, people are dying, Ms. Gentry. If you don't stop poking around, you're going to get killed." He paused, his expression grave. "Now, go home and let me handle this investigation."

Dex didn't comment. But Lamar knew Dex wouldn't back down because of danger.

"What about the homeless men, about Harry?" Melissa asked. "Are you going to investigate what happened to them?"

Lamar crossed his arms. "As a matter of fact, I have

been doing that. I believe your friend Jim Smith is responsible, and McTruitt was onto him. That's why Smith killed McTruitt and ran."

Chapter Nine

Melissa stiffened, the fact that she'd found that bandanna and kept it taunting her. She should show it to Detective Lamar. But it really meant nothing. It might not even belong to Jim Smith.

Lamar seemed so certain Smith was a bad guy. What if she was wrong about him, too? What if he *had* been running from the law?

"What makes you think Jim is killing homeless men when he was one of them?" she asked.

Lamar scratched his chin. "I can't share details of an ongoing investigation. But let's just say that I found evidence McTruitt had gathered that points in that direction."

"Why would Smith kill the homeless?" Dex asked.

Lamar slanted him an irritated look. "Like I said, I can't share details yet. But I do believe he had you fooled, Ms. Gentry."

Melissa's chest squeezed as she remembered the protective glint in Jim's eyes when he'd ordered McTruitt to let her go.

"If McTruitt was following the law and thought Smith was dangerous, then why did he pull a gun on me?" Melissa asked.

"I don't know the answer to that," Lamar said. "Except that he wanted to get Smith out of the shelter and that was the fastest way to do it."

"I just don't think Jim's a cold-blooded killer," Melissa said.

Lamar's look softened. "I'm sorry, Ms. Gentry, but you're wrong. At this point, he's considered a wanted felon, so if you're withholding information or know where he is, you can be charged with conspiracy to commit murder."

Melissa's eyes widened.

"Lamar, ease up," Dex said in a gruff tone. "Melissa spent time with Smith, so maybe she has insight we don't."

Lamar raised a bushy brow. "Listen, Dex, you and I both know that people can be deceptive. Con men are experts at choosing personality types that will buy into their acts." He tilted his head toward Melissa. "I'm sorry, ma'am. You seem like a caring, trusting woman. Unfortunately, that's exactly the type con artists prey on."

Melissa twisted her hands together. The detective was right.

Self-doubt assailed her. She'd attended workshops on the topic and had been taught to not let down her guard. She had been educated in signs to watch for to protect herself and the others who sought help at the shelter.

Had she been wearing blinders around Jim Smith?

TENSION STRETCHED BETWEEN Dex and Melissa as he drove back toward her house. He sensed she was struggling with Lamar's allegations against Smith, so he stopped for an early dinner at a pizza joint a few blocks from Melissa's.

They agreed on a half-veggie, half-meat-lover's pie. He ordered a beer and Melissa joined him. She'd never been the fussy type, and enjoyed a cold one with him on occasion.

Melissa's silence worried him. But they both needed time to assimilate the conversation with Lamar. Questions nagged at him. If Smith was killing the homeless men, what was his motive?

Had he persuaded them to do something illegal for him, then killed them to keep them quiet?

And how did it relate to the vet and his death?

Lamar had suggested greed for bull sperm or prize bulls might have gotten Huckleberry killed. Stealing those and reselling could bring big money—a motive.

If Smith killed McTruitt because the PI was onto whatever scheme he was running, was Smith working with the shooters today?

His father's face flashed back. He'd been living in a shelter. Could his death have been something other than a DUI accident?

Or was he straining for an explanation that didn't exist because he didn't want to believe his father had been drinking and driving?

Melissa pushed her plate away. "Dex, are you okay?"

He gave her a wry smile. "I was going to ask you the same thing."

Melissa gazed down into her drink. "I'm just trying to make sense of everything."

"So am I," Dex admitted. "I keep trying to connect my father's death to all of this because of the shelters." He set his hat on the chair beside him and raked a hand through his shaggy hair. "I saw the empty liquor bottle on the seat beside him. The ME confirmed that his blood alcohol content was off the charts, that he probably passed out and lost control, then his truck nose-dived into the creek."

"But you don't believe that's what happened?" Melissa asked.

Dex shrugged. "How can I know, when I have no idea where my dad has been or what he's been doing?"

"Was he a drinker when he lived at home?"

Bitterness had driven Dex to banish memories of his father for so long that now he struggled to recall details of life with him. "Not really. He had a beer occasionally, but never more than one. Even when Chrissy first went missing and he was really upset, he didn't drink. He was determined to find her, and went out for hours and days at a time spearheading search parties. He promised my mother he'd never give up until he found her."

Melissa squeezed his hand. "I'm sorry, Dex. That must have been a horrible time for your family."

"It was. But it was even worse when he abandoned us."

"He didn't leave a note or contact your mother afterward?"

"Not even once," Dex said.

An awkward silence stretched between them, his heart aching with the memories.

"It's possible the stress caused him to have a psychotic break," Melissa offered. "Or that your father was so overwhelmed with guilt and grief that he couldn't face the family."

"None of us blamed him," Dex said. They'd all been too busy blaming themselves.

Melissa squeezed his hand again. "Maybe not, but he was the father, the patriarch of the family. Most likely he thought it was his job to protect all of you. And when he couldn't, he felt like he'd failed."

The bitterness in Dex's chest wavered. He could understand those feelings. "Maybe. But he should have stuck around for my mom. Losing Chrissy and then him, I don't know how she survived and raised us."

Melissa offered him a smile. "She sounds like an incredibly strong woman."

A myriad of emotions tightened Dex's throat. "She is."

Melissa ran her fingers through her hair. "I always thought I was a good judge of character," Melissa said softly. "Now I'm questioning myself. What if I only saw good in Smith because that's what I wanted to see?"

"He did save your life," Dex said. "I can understand why you'd want to see the good in him."

Her troubled gaze locked with his, tension simmering between them.

"I probably should have told the detective about this." Melissa pulled that red bandanna from her pocket and laid it between them on the table. "I found it caught in the corner of the barn door."

Dex narrowed his eyes. "I don't understand. I thought you said it was nothing."

"It might be nothing." Melissa sighed. "But I think it belonged to Jim Smith."

Dex stiffened. "If that belongs to Smith, then he was at the vet's office. Lamar might be right. Smith could have killed Dr. Huckleberry."

MELISSA WINCED AT the accusation in Dex's voice. "He wasn't the one shooting at us," Melissa said. "It was those other men."

"They could be working together," Dex pointed out.

"I suppose it's possible, but I just don't believe Jim would hurt anyone. There has to be another explanation."

"Melissa," Dex said, his voice hardening. "Maybe you have been fooled by him. If he's involved like Lamar suspects, and he's using these homeless men and killing them, he may be responsible for Harry's disappearance."

Melissa tossed the idea around in her head.

"I'm going to check the medical examiner's report on my father's death, too. Smith could have killed him, then made it appear as if he drank himself into an accident."

Melissa jerked her gaze up to meet his. She hated the pain she saw there. If there was anything she could do to ease it, she would.

But believing his theory meant Jim Smith was a cold-blooded, calculating killer.

She took a deep breath. "If you really think that, then give Detective Lamar the bandanna."

Dex stared at the cloth for a moment, indecision playing across his face. Then he stuffed it in his pocket. "Lamar ordered me to stay out of his way, so I'll have Lucas see if he can lift prints." He paused. "Do you have anything that belonged to Smith that I can use for comparison?"

Melissa rubbed her temple. "He was always writing in these little notepads. He may have left one in his room. Although the detective may have taken it. I can look when I go back into the shelter."

The waitress arrived with their check, and Melissa reached for her wallet, but Dex shook his head. "I've got it."

"Dex—"

"It's just pizza and a beer," Dex said.

Melissa thanked him and gathered her purse, then they walked outside to his SUV. Night had fallen since they'd entered the restaurant, the heat still oppressive. Another night that the shelter was closed meant another night men were without a meal or a bed and a roof over their heads.

Memories of going to bed hungry and sleeping in an alley that reeked of urine and trash taunted her as Dex drove back to her bungalow.

"Hopefully the detective will release the shelter tomorrow," Melissa said. "Then I'll hunt for that notepad."

"Smith's pad may contain information on his plans," Dex said.

"True." Maybe it had proof that would clear Smith of suspicion. For some reason she couldn't put her finger on, he felt like a father figure to her. She didn't want to believe that she'd been wrong about him.

Or that he was a murderer.

DEX FOLLOWED MELISSA up to the door. "I'll check inside to make sure it's secure."

"That's not necessary, Dex," Melissa said.

He gritted his teeth. The fact that she kept defending Smith irritated him. If Smith was guilty, he could come after Melissa and try to use her.

"Humor me," he said gruffly. "You've been shot at several times the last two days. We don't know if we were just in the wrong place, or if someone is watching you, or us."

Fear darted across her face, then she unlocked the door.

"Do you own this house?" he asked as he followed her into a small foyer with hardwood floors that desperately needing refinishing.

"No, it's a rental." Melissa dropped her purse on an accent table near the door. "I don't stay in one place long enough to buy."

On a sofa table behind the faded blue couch, Dex noticed a photograph of a child he assumed was Melissa standing beside an older man. He was thin and dressed in shabby clothes, and so was the little girl. She had one tiny hand in her father's and the other wrapped around the handle of a battered little red suitcase. Her big blue eyes looked haunted and incredibly sad.

"This is you and your father?" he asked.

Melissa nodded. "Yeah, the cook at the shelter where we were staying took the picture before we left one morning. My dad used to say we were going on another adventure. When I was really little, I believed him. But as I got older, I realized we had to keep moving because we either had no money, or our time at the shelter where we were currently staying had run out."

Dex's gaze met hers. Some people would have felt sorry for themselves, or had a chip on their shoulder. Not Melissa. Her mature acceptance raised his admiration even more.

He scanned the open living room and kitchen and

was surprised to see unpacked boxes standing in the corner. "Did you just move in?"

"No, I've been here almost a year."

He studied her. "But you haven't unpacked?"

She shrugged. "I move a lot, so why unpack? Besides, I don't have much anyway."

He was so close to his family, and had lived on or near Hawk's Landing all his life. He couldn't imagine not having a place to hang his hat and call home.

She gestured around the room. "Everything looks fine. No one inside."

"Let me check the rest of the house." Someone could be hiding in a closet.

She looked wary, but didn't argue as he examined the windows. They were locked, but the wood was rotting, the locks flimsy. One windowpane was cracked, which would make it easy for someone to break it and get inside.

A small hall to the side of the kitchen led to a door and a wooden deck that overlooked an overgrown yard. The yard backed up to an alley between streets that looked shady.

Not a safe area.

The door lock was rusty. Anyone with a hairpin could break into that damn door. His boots clicked on the floor as he returned to the kitchen and found a hall bathroom and one bedroom. Melissa's.

A blue-and-white quilt, which looked as if it had been homemade, covered the iron bed.

"One of the ladies at the shelter gave me that quilt when I was young," Melissa said behind him. "It's the only thing that I've kept."

His lungs squeezed for air. Melissa had had a rough childhood but had devoted herself to helping others.

But someone had nearly killed her today.

He crossed the room and surveyed her windows. Same shabby locks. A quick look in the closet revealed nothing but a row of blouses and jeans. No fancy shoes or dresses.

A suitcase sat in the doorway of the closet as if waiting for her to leave again.

"Satisfied?" Melissa asked he walked back to the doorway.

"You need better window locks, and a dead bolt on the front and back door."

"I'll be fine, Dex."

"Do you have a gun?" Dex asked.

Her eyes widened. "No."

"Hang on." Dex hurried outside and returned a minute later with a rifle. "Do you know how to use one of these?"

"Yes, but I'm not sure I could shoot someone."

He gripped her hand and put the rifle into it. "If someone breaks in, you have to defend yourself."

Her face paled.

Dammit, he hated to frighten her, but the thought of leaving her alone was driving him crazy with worry. "Just put it in the closet in case you need it. Please."

She bit down on her lip, then nodded and placed the rifle on the top shelf of her closet.

The strangle marks on her throat taunted him as she faced him again. Anger blended with other emotions he didn't want to think about or name.

He lifted his hand and brushed his fingers across her neck. She sucked in a sharp breath. "Dex?"

"Does it hurt?"

Emotions flared in her eyes. Fear and…an awareness of the two of them standing close together. He breathed in her sweet scent. Rosewater.

Heat flared between them.

Her lips parted on a sigh, and he couldn't help himself. He cupped her face in his big hand and closed his lips over hers.

He needed to feel her in his arms and remind himself that she'd survived tonight.

Chapter Ten

Even as Melissa told herself to pull away from Dex, she leaned into the kiss. His arms slid around her, comforting and strong. His body was hard yet warm, stirring a need in her that had lain dormant since the last time she'd been with him.

His lips felt tender yet a hot hunger laced his kiss, and she wrapped her arms around his neck, savoring the feel of his mouth on hers. He took at the same time he gave, tracing her lips with his tongue until she welcomed him inside.

He threaded his fingers through her hair and groaned. That gruff masculine sound of need aroused her even more. She sighed and raked her hands down his back, and he pulled her hips into the V of his thighs. His hard length nudged her heat, a reminder of the closeness they'd once shared and the emotions being with him had unleashed.

Once she'd given him her body, he'd had her heart.

It would be the same again if she allowed herself to succumb to this passion.

Passion had never been the problem. The passion had always been there, potent and breathing life between them, making it difficult to think about anything but touching and feeling.

It was committing to more that had nearly made her crumble.

She wouldn't crumble this time because she wouldn't allow it to get that far.

Still, she didn't pull away. Lord help her, but she was weak. And it had been so long since anyone had held her.

He deepened the kiss, their lips and tongues dancing together in a sensual rhythm that belonged only to them, as if they had been made for this. For each other.

Dex moved against her, pulling her closer to the sofa, and she complied and raked her hands across his back, clinging to the hard muscles and planes of his broad body. He trailed kisses down her neck and throat, and she tilted her head back on a sigh, offering him access to tease her. And he did. His soft tongue lashes along her skin made her tingle all over.

But just as he reached for the button to her blouse, his phone buzzed. They both startled, then he leaned his head against hers, their ragged breathing echoing in the air between them.

She closed her eyes, willing herself to be strong, to resist the temptation to beg him to forget the phone and make love to her.

He didn't answer it right away. He seemed to be struggling just as she was.

They might be in trouble, have already gone too far.

The phone buzzed again, a harsh reminder of the fact that he was here because he was working a case involving her.

Not to declare his love.

"I'd better get this."

She nodded against him and inhaled a sharp breath as he pulled away. Needing distance and space, she rushed to the bathroom. The woman in the mirror didn't even look like her. Her face was flushed, her hair disheveled, her eyes flaring with need.

Her chest heaved for a breath, her body humming with unsated desire. But it was the stark loneliness in her expression that scared her. She hadn't realized how much she'd wanted to be part of a couple, a family, until she'd met Dex years ago. Or how much she could miss someone when they were gone.

She didn't want to feel that aching emptiness again.

A tear slid down her cheek. No, she could not go back to loving and being left behind. That was the story of her life.

Determined to regain control, she splashed cold water on her face. Dex would leave when he finished investigating. And she would be fine.

Her heart would remain intact.

After all, he couldn't break it if she didn't give it to him.

DEX SILENTLY CURSED as he watched Melissa retreat into her room. She'd needed comfort tonight, but he'd let his own needs interfere and had nearly gone too far.

It couldn't happen again.

His phone buzzed again. He walked to the window and looked out, then checked the number. Officer Whalen, who worked with Lamar. He quickly connected. "Dexter Hawk."

"Detective Lamar asked me to let you know that

we've released Lend-A-Hand so they can clean up and reopen."

"Thanks. I'll pass that information on to the assistant director." Melissa would be happy about the news. "Is there anything you can tell me about the evidence Lamar has against Jim Smith?"

Her exasperated sigh followed. "Mr. Hawk, I'm afraid I can't share information in an ongoing investigation. Perhaps you should speak to Detective Lamar yourself."

Except his friend wasn't in a sharing mood.

Melissa reappeared from the bedroom and stepped into the kitchen as if avoiding him. Her look was wary, and she'd pulled her hair back into a ponytail.

Yeah, he'd definitely gone too far.

The officer hung up, and Dex closed the curtain, then shoved his phone in his pocket. "Lamar released the shelter as a crime scene."

Relief flooded her face. "Good. I'll go over tomorrow and inform the volunteers."

Dex cleared his throat. "Melissa, I'll arrange a crime scene cleanup crew. They're experts at getting out blood."

She winced. "We don't have a budget to pay for cleaning or repairs," Melissa said. "The volunteers and I will handle it ourselves."

"I'll foot the bill," he offered.

"I can't let you do that," Melissa said softly.

Dex squared his shoulders. "Doesn't the center take donations?"

Her gaze met his. "Of course we accept donations."

"Well, consider it a donation, then." He slanted her a grin. "I've dug a few bullets from walls in my time. And I'm pretty good with a hammer."

She laughed softly. "That doesn't surprise me. But I know you're busy with work."

He shrugged. Nothing took priority over protecting her. "I need to know what happened to Harry and these other homeless men."

"I understand." She rubbed her neck, drawing his attention back to the fingerprint marks on her throat where she'd nearly been strangled.

Anger rose inside him again, followed by the temptation to pull her into his arms and kiss those bruises.

The phone had stopped him before. He had to exert self-control now.

"I know you're tired. I'll leave and let you rest." He walked toward the door. "I'll pick you up in the morning and drive you to the center to evaluate the damage."

She agreed, and he opened the door. But that picture of her with her father and that damned little red suitcase taunted him. God, he hated to leave her alone in this dump.

But if he stayed, it would be impossible to keep his hands to himself, so he headed to his SUV.

Dark clouds hovered above, threatening a storm. Rain might cool things, but tonight the air felt steamy.

He scanned the neighboring property, his instincts alert. Two guys in hoodies hovered near a dumpster a block away.

Worry for Melissa mushroomed inside him, and he slid into his SUV, backed out of the driveway, then drove down the street. A rough looking man next door saw him and darted down the alley.

If whoever was behind the shooting learned where she lived, he might send someone else after her. If it was Smith, hell, the man could have followed her home at any time while he stayed at the shelter.

Unable to shake the feeling that she might still be in danger, he parked two doors down from Melissa across the street and decided to watch her house.

MELISSA PACED THE confines of the small house, scrutinizing the interior as Dex must have seen it. Shabby was the word she'd use. Worn and outdated furniture, mismatched kitchen appliances, a beat-up wooden floor and curtains that should have been replaced ten years ago.

She'd done nothing to make it her own. Except for the lone photograph of her and her father, she had no personal items of any kind. No collections or special art or mementos.

Her family consisted of the volunteers and workers at the shelter and the people who sought refuge at Lend-A-Hand.

Material things didn't matter. People did. All she needed was a place to lay her head at night.

That was all she'd ever known.

It had to be enough.

Dex's masculine fragrance lingered in the air, teasing her with what-ifs. What if she could have love and a family, a child, of her own? What if she had a home where she could display family pictures of her baby and the memories they made?

What if she stayed in one place instead of moving around as if on the run herself?

On the run from what?

She'd wondered that about Jim Smith and so many others that joined them at Lend-A-Hand and the other shelters where she'd worked the past decade. Yet she'd never realized how much she was like them.

She moved around so she wouldn't get too attached.

She pressed her fingers to her lips, remembering that kiss. She would be lying if she didn't admit that she wanted it again. That for a second when she'd closed her eyes, she'd fantasized about making love with Dex and waking up in his arms the next morning. And the morning after.

Thankfully, though, he'd left. Tomorrow they'd go to the shelter and get back to business. No more heated kisses.

She walked to the bedroom and glanced at the suitcase she kept in the corner. The urge to pack and find a new start seized her.

But she couldn't leave until she understood what had happened with Smith. And Harry. And if other homeless men were being targeted.

Too antsy to sleep, she snatched her purse and keys and decided to go to the shelter. Jim Smith had constantly written in those little notebooks. But he hadn't had time to retrieve them after the shooting.

Maybe they held something that would help Dex solve the case.

She slipped out the side door and locked it, then rushed to her minivan. It was just as battered as the house. But it served its purpose. It got her around and was big enough to transport supplies to the shelter and from donation centers to alternative housing when necessary. That usually meant a positive step for a person or family. They'd obtained employment and were moving into a home or apartment of their own.

She glanced to the neighbor's drive, grateful it was

dark and the driveway empty. She hadn't shared with Dex her anxiety over the guys next door. She was almost certain they were dealing drugs, but she had no proof. At this point, she couldn't afford to anger them or they might retaliate against her.

She pulled onto the street and drove toward the shelter, keeping alert as she maneuvered the roads. She'd never been paranoid, just careful. After the last two days, she'd be crazy not to be.

Darkness enveloped her, the night a reminder that the house she lived in might need updating, but she had a roof over her head and she was grateful for it. There were others out there less fortunate, sleeping on park benches, or alleys or in their cars.

She turned onto the narrow road leading to Lend-A-Hand, veered into the back parking lot and parked. It seemed odd to see the place dark, closed, empty.

Hope brightened her dismal mood. Tomorrow they could reopen. She scanned the exterior for signs of trouble, then grabbed her flashlight and slid from the van. She clenched her keys as she approached the back entrance, unlocked the door and slipped inside.

The scent of blood lingered. Or maybe it was embedded in her memory. She paused and forced herself to remember that the police had cleared the shelter. It was time to move forward and prove that she wouldn't shut down this place because of one incident.

She eased the door closed, listening for sounds of an intruder, but an eerie quiet reverberated through the space. She fought off her fear and allowed pleasant memories to return. Thanksgiving, when they'd served turkey and dressing, then Christmas, when they'd given wrapped packages of socks and hygiene supplies as gifts. Like a family, they'd worked together to prepare a warm holiday feeling.

Not wanting to alert anyone of her presence in case a vagrant or questionable sort was watching, she used her flashlight to shine a way to the bunk room. She forced herself not to go into the common room where the shooting had occurred.

Smith had occupied a cot in the back left corner of the bunk room, so she passed the other cots, shining her light on the floor. A coin in the corner caught her eye, a battered comb, and a bus ticket stub. All fallen between the cracks of the cots.

She reached Smith's, and shined the light across the mattress. The blanket still lay neatly folded as he'd left it. He had always been neat and orderly. She checked the floor beneath the bed, then raked her hand between the sheet and blanket, and underneath the mattress.

Suddenly a creak of the floor made her freeze. She clenched the flashlight, braced to use it as a weapon if necessary.

But a cold hand grabbed the flashlight, then another hand covered her mouth and the man jerked her against the wall.

Chapter Eleven

Melissa's heart pounded as the man tightened his grip. She'd escaped death twice lately—was this going to be the end for her?

She dug her nails into his arms, struggling to get free.

"I'm not going to hurt you," the man growled in her ear. "Just be still and don't scream, and I'll let you go."

Melissa froze again, the voice registering. Jim Smith?

"Do you understand?" he said in a low voice.

She nodded, her breathing rasping out as he released her. She whirled around, squinting in the darkness.

Yes, it was him. Jim Smith.

The scar on his face made him look menacing in the dark.

Detective Lamar's accusations rang in her head. "What are you doing?" she cried. "And why did you run? I told the police you saved my life."

"It doesn't matter what you told them," Smith said, his voice laced with frustration. "That cop is gunning for me."

Melissa narrowed her eyes. "What does he have against you?"

Smith paced in front of the beds, his limp pronounced, his agitation obvious. "I don't know."

"Please let me call him. We'll explain what happened together. I was a witness."

"You already did that and he's still after me," Smith said. "I'm serious, Melissa. I think that cop wants me dead."

Melissa shook her head in denial. "That can't be true. Why would he want you dead?"

Smith's jaw tightened as his gaze landed on the bruises on her neck. "He's a dirty cop," Jim finally said.

Chilled, Melissa rubbed her arms. "Why would you say that?"

"Because he tried to kill me," Smith said.

"What? When? Where?"

"At that vet's clinic."

Melissa inhaled sharply. "You were there?"

He nodded. "But I didn't kill the vet. I swear. He was dead when I arrived. I saw someone dragging him toward the barn. I hid, but Lamar appeared out of nowhere and shot at me."

Confusion clouded Melissa's mind. "Detective Lamar was there before Dex and I arrived?"

He nodded. "I'm telling you—he's dirty. And he's setting me up."

"None of this makes sense," Melissa said.

Smith wiped his hand over his eyes. "I know. I've been trying to figure out why he'd frame me for murder, but I don't have a clue."

"Then let me call my friend Dexter," Melissa pleaded. "He's a private investigator—"

Smith shook his head. "I saw that Hawk guy with

the detective. Melissa, if they're friends, then you can't trust Hawk."

Melissa's breath caught. She hadn't trusted very many people in her life.

But Dex was the one man in the world she did trust. Occasionally he might cross the line, but he fought for justice.

Still, what if Jim was right and Lamar was dirty?

DEX'S IRRITATION HAD mounted as he followed Melissa to the shelter. Why the hell had Melissa driven here tonight? They'd planned to come together in the morning.

Dammit, didn't she know how dangerous it was to be here alone at this hour?

The interior was dark, but her flashlight beam glowed through the window. Had she simply wanted to see the damage to the place without him hovering over her?

If so, why hadn't she turned on a light?

He slid from his truck and eased up to the side of the building. The light from her flashlight was coming from the back, maybe the bunk rooms?

He crept closer and inched along the wall, then peered through the window.

Cold fear seized him. A man was inside the room with her. He leaned closer. A male voice, one that sounded angry.

Had she stumbled on a vagrant who'd drifted in? Or did she know this man?

He peered closer, trying to discern the man's face. A sliver of moonlight illuminated a deep jagged scar on his cheek, and a nose that had been broken at least twice. He was tall but thin, tattered clothes hanging on his frame as he paced. His left leg must have been injured because he limped as he paced. Thick shaggy silver hair made him look like he was in his fifties maybe sixties, and he was missing a finger on his left hand.

Was it Smith?

Had Melissa intentionally come here to meet him?

According to Lamar, Smith was armed and dangerous. Dex pulled his gun. He couldn't take any chances, not with Melissa's life.

Moving slowly, he eased into the side door and inched down the hall, his gun at the ready. The voices drifted to him, Melissa's soft and hushed, the man's low and rough. He couldn't quite understand what they were saying. Except he did hear Melissa call the man Jim.

It was Smith, dammit.

He gripped his weapon tighter, bracing himself to barter for Melissa's life.

He crept to the doorway, then raised his gun and aimed it inside as he stepped into the entry to the bunk room. Just as he did, the man's hand came up, a gun clenched in it.

"Don't come any closer," Smith growled.

Dex planted his feet firmly, his stance a statement that he didn't intend to back down. "Let her go," Dex said coldly. "If you want a hostage, take me instead."

Their gazes locked in a standoff.

Melissa stepped between them, her hands raised. "Both of you put your guns down. We all have to talk."

"He was holding a gun on you," Dex snapped. "Why should I listen to anything he has to say?"

"He didn't have a gun on me," Melissa said. "We were just talking."

"That cop is framing me," Smith said bluntly. "How

do I know you aren't helping him, that you aren't here to kill me?"

Dex hardened his jaw. "Every criminal claims he was set up."

"I'm not a criminal," Smith said.

"You ran from the law," Dex muttered. "You wouldn't do that if you weren't guilty of something."

"He's not a cold-blooded killer," Melissa interjected before Dex could argue. "He saved my life, Dex. When he took that gun from McTruitt, he could have hurt others at the shelter, but he didn't."

Melissa turned to Smith before Dex could speak. "And Dex is not going to shoot you. He's a good guy, Jim. I trust him. So can you."

Smith's gaze moved from Melissa to Dex, skepticism darkening his eyes. "But he's buddies with that detective."

"Believe me, Jim, Dex just wants justice." She pinned them both with a disgusted look. "Now put down your guns, *both* of you."

Dex and Smith stared at each other for a long moment, the tension thick.

Dex shifted as Melissa gave him an imploring look. "You do trust me, don't you, Dex?"

His lungs squeezed for air. He did trust her. But he didn't trust Smith or any other man where Melissa was concerned.

Smith cleared his throat. "I trust you, Melissa." He slowly lowered his gun, then eased it onto the cot nearest Melissa.

Dex inhaled and did the same. "All right," he said as he stepped away from his weapon. "Now we all know Smith is not your real name. Who the hell are you?"

MELISSA BREATHED A sigh of relief as the men relinquished their weapons. For a moment, she'd feared they'd go at it, if not with guns, with fists. The testosterone and anger in the room was a visceral force.

Dex stepped toward the wall, flipped on a light and seemed to study Smith. "Who are you?" Dex repeated.

Jim's face paled. "That's a question I can't answer."

"Can't or won't?" Dex growled.

"Can't," Jim said in a gruff tone.

Dex crossed his arms. "What does that mean?"

Melissa shot him a warning look. "Jim, tell us what's going on and maybe we can help you."

He glanced back and forth between the two of them, then sank onto one of the cots and scrubbed a hand over his face. He looked wary and exhausted, as if he hadn't slept since the shooting. Maybe he hadn't.

She softened her tone. "Please talk to us."

He cut his gaze toward Dex. "Why? So he can call his dirty cop friend to arrest me?"

"Because we all want the truth," Melissa said. "Dex has been searching for his father who disappeared almost two decades ago. Recently he found him, but he was dead. He traced him to a homeless shelter where he learned that several homeless men have gone missing the past few months."

Jim's brows climbed upward. "I don't understand."

"Me neither," Dex said. "But I think someone is preying on homeless men." Dex paused, voice cold. "Detective Lamar thinks that person is you."

"Me?" Jim flattened his hand on his chest. "Why in the world would he think that?"

"I don't know," Melissa said. "Dex?"

Dex shrugged. "Maybe you should start with who you are and why Clark McTruitt was after you."

Silence fell across the room, filled with Dex's mistrust.

Melissa softened her tone. "Please, Jim, talk to us."

He made a frustrated sound. "I wish I could tell you who I am. My real name. But I don't know what it is."

"Don't bother feeding us some story," Dex said sharply. "Either tell the truth or I will call Detective Lamar."

Jim lifted his head, resignation in his eyes. "I *am* telling you God's honest truth. I have amnesia."

Melissa traded a look with Dex, questions echoing between them. Finally she broke the strained silence. "What happened? Were you in an accident?"

Jim rubbed the back of his head. "A head injury."

"How did you get it?" Dex asked.

Jim stared at the floor, at his boots, his hand tracing a line over his head where a scar must have settled in his hairline. "The last thing I remember was being on some farmland near a bunch of rocks. Someone attacked me and hit me in the back of the head. I blacked out. When I came to, I was disoriented and confused. I didn't remember anything, but my head was hurting and I was bloody. I started walking and eventually found the road." His voice cracked. "Some trucker picked me up and dropped me at a free clinic where they stitched me up. I went from there to a shelter near the clinic, and I've been wandering around ever since trying to figure out what happened, and who I am."

Melissa's heart ached for the man. If his story was true, Jim had been the victim of a violent attack.

And whoever had attacked him might still be after him.

DEX LOCKED HIS teeth together. Melissa was buying Smith's story, hook, line and sinker. He straddled the fence. The man sounded sincere, but amnesia?

It was possible, he supposed.

It was also downright convenient.

"Why was McTruitt after you?" Dex asked again.

Smith raised his gaze, his look flat. "I have no idea. But he's not the first person who's tried to kill me over the years. That's one reason I've stayed on the move."

"Did you have any ID on you when you regained consciousness?" Dex asked.

Smith shook his head. "No, nothing."

"How long were you out?" Dex asked.

Smith shrugged. "I don't know." He touched his hair again. "The blood had dried on the back of my head so it must have been a while."

"How long ago was this?" Melissa asked.

Smith frowned. "Years. Maybe fifteen, sixteen." He rubbed his head again. "Maybe longer. I…sometimes my memory slips. I've lost days, even weeks at times."

"That must be awful," Melissa said softly.

"Where exactly were you were attacked?" Dex asked.

Smith worked his mouth from side to side. "Some farmland or a ranch, I think. It was rugged, miles from a road." He pulled an arrowhead from his pocket and showed it to Dex. "I found this on the ground beside me. There were a lot more arrowheads there, too."

Memories teased at Dex's mind. He and Chrissy searching for arrowheads on Hawk's Landing. She'd loved finding the arrowheads with him. She'd wanted to go hunting for them the night he and his brothers were supposed to watch her. But he hadn't been in the mood. Then he'd told her to get lost.

The guilt made it hard to breathe again.

Melissa cleared her throat. "Jim, you're always writing in those notepads. What's in them?"

Smith released a wary sigh. "Notes of places I go, people I meet. I keep hoping something will ring a bell and trigger my memories to return."

"What have you learned?" Dex asked.

Smith shook his head. "Not much, except that someone wants me dead."

If that were true, there had to be a reason. Several scenarios popped into Dex's mind. Smith had crossed someone the wrong way, he was party to a crime or a witness—and that person wanted to make sure his memories stayed buried.

Chapter Twelve

Dex studied Smith's body language. He'd learned to read people. Typically, if they were lying, they had a tell.

So far, he hadn't detected one with this man. "Where was this shelter where the driver dropped you?"

"About a half hour from here. Doc said I had a concussion and told me to rest for a few days."

"How long did you stay there?" Dex asked.

Smith shrugged. "A couple of weeks. Thought my memory might come back, but nothing. Then I kept getting this antsy feeling like someone was watching me. That's when I left. Been doing that ever since."

"Did you see someone or notice a particular car?" Dex asked.

Smith shook his head. "Not anyone I could identify. But sometimes I'd see a dark car following me." He rubbed the back of his head again. "Maybe I was paranoid because of my head injury, but I figured if someone left me for dead and found out I survived, they might come back and finish the job." He hesitated, voice shaky. "I got shot at outside Dallas once. And then in Austin another time." He wrung his hands together. "And then that guy broke into Lend-A-Hand and put a gun to Ms. Melissa's head."

"And you defended her?" Dex asked, tensing.

Smith rubbed at his leg as if it was hurting. "Had to. The man wanted me. I couldn't let him hurt Ms. Melissa. She's the kindest person I've ever met."

Dex couldn't argue with that. "How about the man who gave you a ride when you first regained consciousness? Do you know his name or where he lives?"

"No. I was pretty out of it that day. Had a killer headache and was so confused I didn't know where I was or where I was going."

"That sounds awful," Melissa said softly.

Smith offered her a tentative smile. "You can't imagine. I feel like I've got a big hole in my head. For a while I wondered if I had family, had hoped someone was looking for me. I searched for pictures in the paper and the news, but never saw any." He gave a low whistle. "I figured if I was a wanted criminal, my picture would be all over the news, too. But it never showed up anywhere."

"Which leads us back to the question—why would someone want you dead?" Dex asked.

"Beats the hell out of me," Smith muttered.

"Did you check the news for crimes that happened around that time?" Melissa asked. "Maybe you witnessed one."

"I checked," Smith said. "But there weren't any major stories. And nothing rang a bell."

Melissa glanced at Dex for answers, but he had none. "Listen, Smith," Dex said, "if you really want to know who you are, I have an idea."

His look turned skeptical. "What?"

"Let me run your prints. If they pop in relation to a past crime or a missing persons' report, it'll give us your name."

Smith shook his head. "That detective friend of yours will lock me up. I'm telling you—he's dirty."

Dex gritted his teeth. He'd known Lamar for nearly two decades. How could he believe a stranger over his friend?

Yet he'd seen Lamar cross the line before. Both times he'd planted evidence that had helped convict his collar.

But both times he'd been certain the perp was guilty and dangerous, and he hadn't wanted the suspects to escape on a technicality.

What kind of evidence did he have against Smith? Lamar hadn't wanted to share with Dex...

"I'll have someone else run the prints and Lamar won't know," Dex offered. Lucas could handle it without involving the Austin PD.

Smith reluctantly agreed. "I guess if I have done something bad, it's time I face it and pay up. If not, maybe I'll finally figure out who I am, and why someone wants to kill me."

"Let me make a call." Dex stepped into the hallway, phoned Lucas and explained the situation.

"You're harboring a fugitive?" Lucas asked in an incredulous voice.

Dex silently counted to ten. "Not exactly. Melissa claims he only acted in self-defense, and Smith insists that Lamar is framing him."

Lucas grunted. "Why would Lamar do that?"

"That's what I'm trying to figure out. Anyway, after hearing Smith's story, I'm beginning to wonder myself."

"What *is* his story?" Lucas asked.

Dex relayed everything Smith had told him, and his suspicions that someone was using homeless men, then killing them.

Lucas hissed. "You've certainly made connections where no one else has."

Dex didn't like the patronizing tone in his brother's voice.

"I may be wrong," Dex said. "But, if I'm not, a predator is targeting the homeless because they don't think anyone will notice or pay attention. Even when they're reported missing, the cops don't prioritize the case because—"

"Because by nature of being without a home or family, the men move around," Lucas said matter-of-factly.

"Right. Just indulge me, Lucas. If we discover Smith has committed a crime, I'll bring him to you myself."

Lucas released an exasperated sigh. "All right. What do you want me to do?"

"Simple," Dex said. "Run his prints without alerting the Austin police. If we learn his identity, we'll go from there."

"And if he is a criminal, you'll turn him over."

"Yes." That was a promise he'd keep. Although he had a feeling Melissa would fight him on it.

And if Smith wasn't a criminal, it was possible that he was a victim just as the other missing homeless men were.

MELISSA'S HEART HURT for Jim Smith. She couldn't imagine what it was like to go through life not knowing who you were or where you came from or if you had any family. Although if he did have family, surely they would have been looking for him. Unless they thought he was dead...

Then again, she'd worked in the system long enough to know that when a family filed a missing persons' report, the police investigated—for a little while. Then other cases took priority, leads went cold and enthusiasm waned.

Eventually the family members accepted the loss, especially if they thought their loved one had left of his or her own accord. Missing children were a different story. Families never really gave up looking for them or hoping for their safe return.

"Why did you come here tonight?" Jim asked her.

Melissa traced a finger over her neck, a chill invading her. "After what happened at the vet's clinic today, I couldn't sleep. I remembered that you kept notepads and came here looking for one. I thought you might have jotted down something important."

Smith patted his shirt pocket. "I usually write down anyone I talk to, especially if I think they might give me useful information."

"Did you know a man named Bill Small or Harry Willis? They were staying at the Retreat Shelter."

He wrinkled his brow. "I haven't been to that one."

Her stomach twisted with unease. Was he holding back?

"Jim, I went to bat for you with Dex. Please be honest with me."

He removed a pad from his pocket and flipped it open. He tapped a page where he'd written the vet's name.

"One night at an old warehouse, I heard some of the men talking about that vet, how he took care of stud bulls. When I regained consciousness years ago, I had a card in my pocket with the name of a cattle breeder on it. I thought if the vet worked with that breeder, he might remember me."

"That's the reason you were at Dr. Huckleberry's today?" Melissa asked.

Smith nodded.

"What happened when you got there?" Melissa asked.

"Those gunmen were dragging the vet's body into the barn. One of them said something about taking care of Harry, then the other guy saw me and fired. I ran for cover. I guess that's when I dropped the bandanna."

"Did you recognize the men or their voices?"

He shook his head. "No, I wish I had. But that detective showed up and fired at me, too, and I had to get the hell out of there."

Dex appeared at the doorway with a scowl. Judging from his expression, he'd overheard their conversation. "I thought you said you didn't have any ID on you when you regained consciousness."

"I didn't," Smith said. "This was a business card." He removed it from his pants pocket and offered it to Dex. "It had the name of a cattle breeder on it. I thought it probably didn't mean anything, but went to talk to him."

"What happened?" Dex asked.

"It was a dead end. The man claimed he had no idea who I was. Said he passed his cards out all the time. I could have picked it up at a ranch or restaurant or rodeo."

"But you kept the card all this time?"

Smith nodded. "I don't know why. But it was all I had to go on."

Melissa saw the wheels turning in Dex's mind. "What is it, Dex?"

"That breeder's name was on a flier in the vet's office." Dex drummed his fingers on his thigh. "It might not be related, but I'm going to question this guy myself."

Jim stood. "I'll go with you."

"No." Dex held up a warning hand. "I'm sticking out my neck for you with my brother. You need to lay low. Stay here and out of trouble. If the police discover Melissa is allowing you to stay here, she'll be arrested for harboring a fugitive."

"I don't want to get her in trouble," Smith said.

"Then let me do the grunt work." Dex took the card from Smith. "One way or the other, I'll get to the bottom of this mess."

DEX HOPED HE wasn't making a mistake in trusting Smith. But he did trust Melissa, and if there was any truth to Smith's story—and to his allegations against Lamar, which Dex did not want to believe—he couldn't stop digging.

He'd give that card to Lucas and see if he could lift a print. If Smith was in the system and dangerous, he'd get the man away from Melissa.

"I'll leave my car here and ride with you," Melissa offered.

Dex shook his head. "It's been a harrowing day, Melissa. Go home and rest. I'll let you know what I learn."

Melissa looked hesitant but agreed, and Dex insisted on walking her to her car.

"Thank you for trusting me and listening to him," Melissa said as he opened her minivan door.

He tightened his jaw. Trust didn't come easy. The one man he'd completely trusted had abandoned him and his family. And now this man he barely knew was making allegations that Lamar, the man who'd mentored him, was dirty. "Just be careful around Smith. Don't let your guard down, Melissa."

Melissa squeezed his arm, tension simmering between them, a reminder of the kiss they'd shared earlier and where it might have taken him.

Dammit. He missed having her in his arms. Although he'd been with other women over the years, no one triggered his emotions the way Melissa did.

But most of all, he missed her sweet smile. If heaven had angels, Melissa Gentry was one of them.

He didn't deserve an angel.

"I'll follow you home and make sure your house is secure." But this time he wouldn't go inside. That would be too dangerous. Too tempting.

"You don't have to do that, Dex. I've been taking care of myself my entire life."

That made him even sadder. She not only took care of herself. She took care of everyone else.

It was time someone took care of her for a while.

"I'm following you," he said bluntly.

Her gaze locked with his, heat flaring.

But she didn't touch him again. She climbed in the minivan, closed the door and started the engine. He hurried to his SUV. He glanced back at the shelter just before he pulled away, and saw Smith hovering in the shadows, watching.

Something about that man disturbed him. Made the hair on the back of his neck stand up.

He needed to figure out what it was. If he was lying and using Melissa and him, he'd put an end to it.

No one would hurt Melissa while he was around.

Chapter Thirteen

Dex conducted another quick search of Melissa's house after he followed her home. Satisfied she was safe for the moment, he hurried away before he succumbed to temptation and asked if he could spend the night.

He paused in the driveway, grabbed his laptop and researched Emmet Wilson. The cattle breeder had an impressive website detailing his expertise and breeding techniques, complete with photographs of prize cattle he'd bred and testimonials from ranchers who'd used his services.

All positive, which made him wonder if the man only allowed positive reviews.

Dex skimmed for details. Wilson utilized natural services along with artificial insemination, genomic-enhanced EPDs, or Expected Progeny Differences, timed estrus synchronization, embryo transfer and sexed semen. He'd also been working with the newest tool, gene editing.

The man owned a large ranch about forty miles from Austin. Night had set in, and the country roads were deserted as he passed small farms and houses on his way. At one time when he was little, his father had talked about expanding his herd at Hawk's Landing.

"4 for 4" MINI-SURVEY

We are prepared to **REWARD** you with 4 FREE books and Free Gifts for completing our MINI SURVEY!

You'll get up to...

4 FREE BOOKS & FREE GIFTS

just for participating in our Mini Survey!

Get Up To 4 Free Books!

Dear Reader,

IT'S A FACT: if you answer 4 quick questions, we'll send you 4 FREE REWARDS from each series you try!

Try **Harlequin Intrigue® Larger-Print** books featuring heroes and heroines that confront and survive danger while finding themselves irresistibly drawn to one another.

Try **Harlequin® Romantic Suspense** books featuring heart-racing sensuality and the promise of a sweeping romance set against the backdrop of suspense.

Or **TRY BOTH!**

I'm not kidding you. As a leading publisher of women's fiction, we value your opinions... and your time. That's why we are prepared to reward you handsomely for completing our mini-survey. In fact, we have 4 Free Rewards for you, including 2 free books and 2 free gifts from each series you try!

Thank you for participating in our survey,

Pam Powers

READER SERVICE—Here's how it works:

Dex and his brothers had ridden with him to an auction house and watched as his father bid for the best deal.

Dex had been infatuated with the auction process and the speed with which the bids were made. His father had studied the cattle from the auction catalog in advance so he was prepared to make the best choice for the ranch.

He was on the verge of expanding the herd when Chrissy went missing. But he'd put those plans on hold while he spearheaded the search parties day and night.

When he hadn't come home that last morning, his mother had assumed he was still out searching. Dex's father had been obsessive about not giving up and had spent long hours combing different parts of the ranch and area by the swimming hole.

By day two, his mother was frantic that something bad had happened to him.

She'd called the sheriff who'd issued a bulletin for his father and his truck, but nothing had turned up. No phone calls. No message or word. No sign of him anywhere.

Emotions flooded Dex, the memories as painful and vivid as if it had happened yesterday.

He blinked and scrubbed a hand over his eyes, then spotted the sign for Wilson's Breeding.

He veered onto the narrow, paved road that led to the main area of the property. A traditional ranch home sat on a hill overlooking the barns and stables spread across the land.

Dex parked in front of the house. As he left the truck and headed to the front door, the sound of cows mooing drifted in the hot air. Once his father left, his mother had slowly sold off their stock. She and her teenage boys couldn't keep up the business, and none of their hearts were into the ranch.

Lately, with the addition of the foster girls, he and Brayden had added horses, and had offered riding lessons to the teens.

The door opened, jarring him back to reality. A short robust man with graying hair and reading glasses perched on the end of his bulbous nose stood in the entry.

"Mr. Wilson?" Dex asked.

"Yeah. What can I do for you?"

Dex removed the business card from his pocket and handed it to the man. "By now, I'm sure you heard about the shooting at the Lend-A-Hand Shelter."

Wilson pushed his glasses up with a crooked thumb. "Yeah. Some guy named Smith. Heard the police are looking for him."

"That's right." Dex studied the man but Wilson showed no reaction to Smith's name. "Smith had his card with you. He said he came to see you a while back. He claims he has amnesia and thought you might know his name."

Wilson cut his eyes to the side and seemed to mull over the information. "I do recall some fellow stopping by saying he didn't know who he was, but that was a long time ago."

Dex nodded. "He also claims someone is trying to kill him." He showed Wilson a photo on his phone. "This is Smith. Maybe you can take another look and something will ring a bell."

Bushy eyebrows raised, Wilson leaned forward and studied the picture. "Can't say it does. But I meet a lot of folks in my business. I could have met him at an auction and don't recall it. Or he could have picked up my card at one. I also visit the rodeos and I work with a vet named Dr. Huckleberry. He keeps cards in his office to hand out to interested clients."

Frustration filled Dex. He was getting nowhere.

"Did you talk to Dr. Huckleberry?" Wilson asked. "Maybe he knows this guy Smith."

Dex shifted. "Actually, I went to see him earlier, but I'm afraid he was dead."

Wilson's eyes widened. "Huckleberry is dead? God... How?"

Wilson's reaction seemed sincere. "He was in the stall with one of the bulls and had been gored. But two men were there and shot at me, so it's possible he was murdered, and they put him in with the bull to cover it up."

The color drained from Wilson's face. "Good Lord. Poor guy." He scratched his chin. "Do you have any idea who'd do such a thing?"

Dex shook his head. "I was hoping you could tell me that."

MELISSA WAS ACCUSTOMED to living alone, but the rental house felt empty now. She missed Dex. His masculine scent lingered, taunting her with the fact that their earlier kiss had almost led to the bedroom.

She phoned April to inform her that they could get in the shelter the next day to reopen. April offered to relay the news to the other volunteers and to Another Chance Shelter. The men she and Dex had transported there could return to Lend-A-Hand if they wanted.

Melissa rolled her shoulders, her muscles aching.

The red marks on her throat were turning dark purple now.

Shivering with the memory of her attacker's hands around her neck, she undressed and showered, letting the warm water soothe her frazzled nerves.

She closed her eyes, savoring the scent of rosewater in her body wash, and scrubbed her body and hair clean. Willing the water to wash away the haunting memories of nearly dying twice, she stood beneath the spray until the water started to turn cold.

Finally, she dried off and pulled on a T-shirt and pajama shorts, then padded to the kitchen and made a cup of hot tea. She needed to sleep and to forget about how close she'd come to death.

Dex could distract her…

Her suitcase caught her eye, but she fought the instinct to pack and run. She couldn't leave yet. Not until she knew what had happened to Bill's friend Harry, or who Jim Smith really was. Or if the shootings and the vet's death and the missing homeless men were connected.

Dex wanted answers about his father, too. She wanted them for him.

Then she would leave town and find a place to start all over again like she had so many times before.

A place where she could permanently put her fantasies about Dexter Hawk behind her.

"Mr. Wilson, do you have any idea why someone would want to kill Dr. Huckleberry?"

Wilson fidgeted and glanced past Dex. "I have no idea. Everyone I know liked the doc."

"Were you two friends?" Dex asked.

Wilson shrugged. "More like business acquaintances. He treated my animals. I respected that and paid him well for it."

"Did he have any enemies?"

Wilson blinked rapidly and shoved his glasses on the top of his head, making his graying hair stick out. "Not that I was aware of. He was married once, but his wife ran off a couple of years ago." He arched a brow. "You think she'd do something like this?"

"I don't know," Dex said. "Was their relationship tumultuous?"

Wilson shrugged again. "Huckleberry worked all the time. She got lonely, entertained herself elsewhere if you know what I mean."

So she'd cheated on him. But that would have given the vet motive to hurt her, not the other way around. "How about financially?"

"Hell, she wanted everything, but he fought her."

"That's certainly a theory the police will investigate," Dex said, although he couldn't imagine a woman dragging her husband into a stall with a raging bull. Then again, she could have hired those men to kill her husband, and he and Melissa showed up at the wrong time.

He made a mental note to ask Lamar about the man's will and if his wife had an alibi. He could check into her financials.

"Or, hell, maybe someone broke in and wanted to steal drugs," Wilson suggested.

"That's another possibility," Dex agreed.

"Did Dr. Huckleberry keep bull sperm at his place?" Dex asked.

Wilson shook his head. "No, the seed we use is locked away tight and secure."

Dex retrieved the recent picture of his father. "Mr. Wilson, one more question. Do you recognize this man?"

Wilson examined the picture. A shake of his head accompanied his response. "Don't know him. Like I said, though, I could have met him at an auction. They draw a crowd."

Dex swallowed disappointment, then assessed the photo of his father taken twenty years ago. "How about this man?"

Another look, then Wilson's gaze rose to his. "Don't think so. Why? You think these men have something to do with Dr. Huckleberry's death?"

"Maybe," Dex said. "Although they didn't kill him. These two photos are of the same man. And he's dead."

"Who is he?" Wilson asked.

"My father, Steven Hawk. He went missing about eighteen years ago. I'm trying to find out what happened to him."

Wilson looked confused at the change of topic. "Are you one of the Hawks who own that big spread, Hawk's Landing?"

"Yes, sir, that's my family."

Wilson grunted. "Sorry I can't help you out more with your questions. But if your family needs any breeding or studs, let me know."

Dex bit back a retort. Wilson might claim he knew nothing, but even under fire, he was pushing his business. Still, he seemed nervous about the vet's murder.

Did he know more than he'd admitted?

MELISSA HAD STRUGGLED with insomnia since she was little. Living on the streets and in shelters had taught her to always keep one eye and ear open for trouble. Dangers lurked everywhere.

Bad men. Drug addicts. Pimps. Thieves. Vandals. Pedophiles.

She hadn't known at the time what that last word meant, only that some men liked little girls. Even inebriated, her father had kept her close for protection.

It was the one honorable thing he'd done.

She tried to put memories of those nights aside as she crawled into bed. But they plagued her in the night.

She was five-years-old. She clenched her raggedy doll to her chest as she stumbled along after her father. He hugged his brown bag to him like it was his lifeline, sipping from the bottle inside.

He called it his liquid courage. Said he needed it to get through the day.

She hated the stinky smell, and the way it made him forget things sometimes. Like where they were going or that they hadn't eaten all day. That he got sloppy and fell and sometimes they didn't make it to the shelter. They'd sleep in the park, which she didn't mind as much as the dirty alleys where it smelled like rotten food and nasty beer and pee.

She saw men relieving themselves as if the alley was their toilet, and always covered her eyes. She didn't like the way they looked at her, as if she was doing something wrong, not them.

A grungy man in an army-green coat unzipped his pants and smiled at her as if he was going to show off his thing. She turned her face into her daddy's sleep-

ing body and hid her eyes, burrowing into him as tight as she could get.

The next day when she'd told him about it, he'd gotten mad. Then he'd dragged her to a shelter and left her by herself. Said little girls didn't belong on the street.

She'd cried and begged him not to leave her with strangers, but he'd shaken off her hands and walked away.

That night she'd lain on the cot alone and stared at the ceiling, willing him to come back. She'd heard noises outside, loud voices. Arguing.

The walls shook and the door bust open...

SHE JERKED AWAKE, trembling, her senses on edge. A noise. She heard it outside.

The window rattled. A banging. Wood creaking.

Fear bolted through her.

Someone was trying to break in.

Chapter Fourteen

Dex decided to stop by the hospital before heading home. The doctors should have had time to treat Melissa's attacker.

Maybe he'd be awake by now.

Normally he'd trust Lamar to call him. But with Lamar's warning, he didn't expect to be looped in on the investigation until Lamar was ready to tie it up.

He drove straight to the hospital and parked, then went inside to the ER. He recognized one of the nurses and approached her.

She was in her midforties, with a passel of kids at home. The plump, tenderhearted woman treated all of her patients as if they were her children, too. She'd assisted the doctors in stitching him up a couple of times when he'd been injured on cases.

He quickly explained that he'd witnessed the shooting and fudged slightly, implying he was working with the police. "Was the man moved to a room?"

She checked the records. "Yes, third floor."

"He was unconscious with no ID when he was admitted," Dex said. "Do you know his name now?"

She shook her head. "Afraid not. A detective named

Lamar put a detail on his room. Haven't you talked to him?" she asked with an eyebrow raise.

"At the crime scene, yes," Dex replied. "But I had a couple of other leads to look into so haven't spoken to him in the last hour." He thanked her with a smile. "I'll go upstairs and see if the man has regained consciousness."

Her phone was buzzing on her hip, and she gestured to it, so he headed toward the elevator. A siren wailed outside, and an ambulance rolled up, sending nurses and doctors scurrying.

He slipped into the elevator and rode it to the third floor, then got off.

Dex checked the room numbers and veered to the right. Voices echoed from the nurses' station on the corner, and people rushed down the hall. A Code Red blasted over the intercom, and a nurse wheeled a crash cart toward the door where nurses and doctors had gathered.

His instincts kicked in, and he picked up his pace. A guy in scrubs rushed past him, heading toward the elevator. Dex moved on, his pulse hammering as he neared the room.

The code was in Room 312, the room where his John Doe was.

A uniformed officer stood at the door, on guard, his face strained as a doctor ushered him out of the way.

"What's happening?" Dex asked as he reached the officer.

The officer shrugged, his stance tense. "Don't know. I went to take a leak, came back, and the prisoner was struggling for air. I pushed the call button and all hell broke loose."

Dex tensed as he watched the nurses and doctors scrambling to try to save the bastard. One doctor was doing CPR, his movements steady. The nurse with the crash cart rushed in, pulled out the paddles and shocked him. The man's body jerked, but the steady beep of the machine beside him indicated he had no pulse.

More voices. The doctor ordering them to do it again.

Another shock. Then another. Then another, each time more intense. The man's body jerked and fell back against the bed, no sign of breathing or life.

A nurse checked the clock. Read the time. Looks were exchanged. Then the doctor put the paddles aside and pronounced the man dead.

Dex cursed beneath his breath. That bastard might have had the answers he needed.

But now he was just another body added to the count. They were piling up fast.

And he was no closer to learning the truth.

MELISSA CLENCHED THE sheets and listened. Outside, the wind was silent. No storm.

The noise…the back door rattling. Someone trying to turn the doorknob.

Her lungs squeezed for air.

What if it was another shooter connected to the vet's death?

Slowly she reached for her phone on the nightstand. She pressed 9-1-1 as she slipped from bed, and ducked into the closet.

"9-1-1, how may I assist you?"

"This is Melissa Gentry. Someone is trying to break

into my house." She quickly gave the operator her address.

"Please stay on the line—"

Melissa shoved the phone into the pocket of her pajama bottoms and snatched the rifle Dex had given her from the closet. Her fingers trembled as she gripped it.

The noise grew louder. The door rattling. She tiptoed into the hallway. A few steps toward the kitchen and she stared at the back door. The knob was definitely turning.

Through the glass in the upper part of the door, a shadow hovered outside, jiggling the doorknob.

Fear nearly paralyzed her. Would the police get here in time?

She pressed her back against the wall, forcing herself to remain still so the intruder couldn't see her through the glass.

Suddenly the window shattered. She trembled and raised the rifle.

A gloved fist shot through the broken glass, clearing shards of glass, then he reached inside and tried to unlock the door.

She stepped closer, close enough she thought the intruder could see her through the opening. He was a big guy, broad shoulders.

She aimed the gun dead center at the man's chest. Then she cleared her throat. "Go away or I'll shoot!"

She held her breath, praying he'd back down. But the door burst open and the man lunged at her. She tried to get off a shot, but he jerked her arm up and the round hit the ceiling. Plaster rained down and she struggled to hold on to the weapon, but he slammed her backward against the wall. Her head hit the wood so hard that the world spun.

Calling on moves she'd learned in a self-defense class, she brought her knee up and aimed for his crotch. He dodged the blow and clawed at the rifle. Another bullet dislodged and hit the wall. She screamed and shoved at him, but he was too strong.

He growled and backhanded her across the face. Her head snapped back, and her control on the gun slipped.

He snatched the rifle from her hands, then flung her across the room. She grappled for control, but her head hit the corner of the wall, and she slid to the floor.

She blinked through blurry eyes and tasted blood.

But she couldn't give up. She crawled to her knees, desperate to see what he looked like. Burly. A beard. Shaggy hair. Dark clothes. A scar across his cheek.

He aimed the rifle at her.

Her life flashed behind her eyes. She'd done good by helping others.

But she wanted more. She wanted love. A family of her own. A real home that she'd never had.

He took a step closer, his menacing expression sending a shiver through her.

Dear God, she didn't want to die…

Dex wanted to slam his fist against the wall. Everywhere he turned, he hit a dead end.

"Was anyone in the room with the prisoner before he coded?" Dex asked.

The officer shrugged. "Just the staff. A nurse earlier. The man seemed fine. Just sleeping." He paused and rubbed his chin as if thinking. "Later, a male nurse came in. Put something in the guy's IV. I figured it was pain meds."

Suspicions rose in Dex's mind. That IV could have held something that killed the man.

The doctor appeared at the doorway, wiping perspiration from her damp forehead. "I'm sorry, Officer. He didn't make it."

"What happened?" Dex asked.

The doctor narrowed her eyes at Dex. "Are you family, sir?"

Dex shook his head. "No, but—"

"I can't discuss this with you," the doctor said. "Either get his family here or I'll talk with the detective in charge."

The doctor's phone was ringing. She answered it, then rushed to a room across the hall.

The officer guarding the room stepped aside to phone Lamar. Dex turned to the nurse. "Did you find out his name?"

She shook her head. "There'll be an autopsy. Maybe the ME can give you insight into his identity."

And an exact cause of death.

The image of the male in scrubs he'd passed rushing toward the elevator surfaced, and Dex hissed. If those scrubs were a disguise, the man could have slipped something in that IV to cause the suspect to have a heart attack.

Inside the room, the doctor had covered the suspect with a sheet and the machines had stopped beeping, the silence eerie.

A minute later, the officer returned, his face stoic. "Detective Lamar said you need to stay away from here."

Dex worked his mouth from side to side. "I just want answers."

The officer attached his phone back on his hip. "Maybe so. But he asked if you'd been in to visit this man. Said you had reason to want him dead."

"Lamar implied that I killed him?"

"Not in those words."

Anger churned inside Dex. Lamar knew him better than that. But this officer? "You've been here since he was brought in?"

"Yes."

"Then you know that I haven't been inside the damn room."

Furious, Dexter walked away. But he dialed Lamar as he rode the elevator. Lamar answered immediately.

"What's going on?" Dex asked. "You think that I did something to the John Doe in the hospital. I wanted—"

"Whoa," Lamar said. "I never said anything of the sort."

"Well, your officer implied it."

A grunt echoed back. "You know how cops are, Dex. Always questioning everything."

"Well, someone may have killed the guy, but it sure as hell wasn't me. I passed a man in scrubs rushing past the elevator as I headed down the hall toward our prisoner. The officer said a male nurse gave the prisoner drugs through an IV. He assumed it was pain meds, but what if someone was disguised as a nurse and killed him?"

"Can you describe this nurse?" Lamar asked.

Dex pinched the bridge of his nose, struggling to recall details. "Probably thirties, clean-shaven, medium build. I didn't get a good look at his face. Talk to your officer. Maybe he can add something."

Lamar mumbled something Dex didn't quite catch. "I'll talk to the officer about it. And I'll make sure the ME conducts a thorough autopsy and reports directly back to me."

"Also, I found out that the vet was divorced. You might want to look into her and see if she was included in Dr. Huckleberry's will."

"Dammit, Dex. I don't need you to tell me how to do my job." Lamar paused. "Hang on. I have to answer this call."

The elevator doors opened, and Dex stepped into the hallway, then walked outside.

Lamar returned on the line just as Dex reached the parking lot.

"Listen, Dex, 9-1-1 just received a call from your friend Melissa." A siren wailed. "I'm headed to her house now."

Dex bolted for his SUV. "I'll meet you there."

He jumped inside his vehicle, started the engine and sped onto the road. He shouldn't have left Melissa alone. What if someone had gotten to her this time and he lost her for good?

MELISSA STARED INTO the man's cold eyes, willing him not to kill her. "Why are you doing this?" she asked. "Why kill me? I don't even know you."

His expression darkened, and he tightened his grip on the rifle. He was younger than she'd thought before. Maybe thirties. He looked rough, too, like he hadn't shaved or had a bath in days. And a knife was sticking out of his pocket.

"If you want money, take whatever I have. It's not much, but it's yours."

He kept the rifle aimed on her, but he quickly scanned the hallway.

"Or if you need help, I'll help you. I work at a shelter," she said, hoping to reach him on some level. "I can offer you a bed to sleep in and food, and if you want, I'll help you find a job."

He barked a laugh. "Shut up, lady."

Her head was starting to throb from the blow he'd given her. "I really want to help you," she said softly. "Please put the gun down."

The rifle wavered slightly, and she thought he was about to lower it. But a siren wailed outside, then flashing blue lights twirled and danced through the window.

Rage and panic shot through his eyes, and he snatched her arm. A loud pounding echoed from the front door.

Then something slammed against the side of her head. The rifle?

She grasped for control. But pain ricocheted through her temple and she felt herself falling into the darkness.

Chapter Fifteen

Dex sped onto the highway and wove through traffic. Although it was nearly 11:00 p.m., locals and tourists were still leaving restaurants and bars. The music scene in Austin drew crowds and fueled the economy. He had his favorite haunts, too.

He'd like to take Melissa to them sometime.

Fear for her made sweat break out on his forehead, and he pressed the accelerator and maneuvered past cars, then turned down a side street to avoid more congestion.

Lamar was on his way to Melissa's. She'd managed to call 9-1-1. Hopefully that was a good sign.

It had to be. The thought of anything bad happening to her felt like a knife tearing into his gut.

He whipped the SUV toward Melissa's street, his pulse hammering at the sight of the police car. Lamar had beaten him here.

He swerved into the drive, scanning the property for trouble in case Lamar needed help. He quickly checked his weapon, but kept it tucked into his belt as he slid from his vehicle and approached the house.

The front door was closed, a light burning from the back of the house. Praying Melissa was safe, he hurried toward the rear side door. It stood ajar, a thin stream of light glowing from the interior.

He inhaled sharply and crept up the stairs, still alert in case Lamar had walked into an ambush and needed backup. He paused at the door to listen for voices or signs of violence, but inside it was quiet.

Too quiet.

With one hand on his weapon, ready to pull it, he inched forward, then peered through the open doorway. A creak of the floor made him hesitate, then suddenly the barrel of a gun appeared in his face.

A second later, Lamar whirled in front of him.

"Whoa, it's me," Dex growled.

Lamar cursed and lowered the gun, his face half hidden in the shadows. "Hell, Dex, you just about got yourself shot."

"I thought you might need help," Dex snapped.

"Sorry." Lamar wiped a hand over his face. "Didn't hear you."

"Where is she? Is she okay?" He didn't wait for a response. He pushed past Lamar to look inside and halted.

A rifle on the floor. Blood splattered on the wall. Melissa's?

Please, God, no.

He inched forward. A look to the left. A man's body was sprawled on the floor, blood pooling beneath his chest, his eyes wide and vacant.

"I got the bastard," Lamar said.

"What about Melissa?"

Lamar gestured toward the right.

Melissa lay on the floor, too, blood seeping from her forehead.

"I called an ambulance," Lamar said.

Dex barely heard Lamar. His heart was hammering so loud the blood was roaring in his ears.

He crossed to Melissa and knelt beside her, then checked for a pulse. He held his breath, waiting. Praying.

Finally he felt it.

She was alive.

For a second, he dropped his head forward and said a prayer of thanks. Swallowing against the emotions clogging his throat, he gently stroked a strand of blood-tinged hair from her cheek. "You're going to be okay, darlin'."

He lifted her head and pulled her in his lap and pressed a kiss to her cheek. "Hang in there. I'm going to take care of you. No one is going to hurt you again."

He hugged her, clinging to her as if she might die if he let go.

Finally, the sound of a siren. The ambulance arriving.

He cut Lamar a look and saw his friend watching him with interest. Typically he didn't wear his emotions on his sleeve. He'd learned to silence them, banish them around other people. Look cold. Hard. Tough.

He couldn't help himself now. He was terrified.

And for the first time in his life, he didn't care if anyone saw it. "What happened?" he asked.

"She was unconscious when I arrived," Lamar said. "Bastard was standing over her with a gun. He fired at me, but I hit him first."

Dex nodded. "Thanks. I owe you."

Lamar's gaze met his, dark and troubled. "Just doing my job."

Maybe so. But he'd saved Melissa tonight. Dex would forever be indebted to him for that.

MELISSA FELT AS if she was floating in an endless sea of black. Something hard was hammering at her skull, beating at her to stay down. To give up and let the emptiness swallow her so the pain would stop.

Instinct whispered for her to fight. She had something important to do. Someone to see. A life to live. Dreams to follow.

All the things she'd never had awaited. She reached out her hand and tried to latch onto them, but they slipped between her fingertips and floated away like dust in the wind.

Voices echoed from the distance. Far away, but occasionally a word sifted through. A familiar gruff voice murmuring her name.

"Melissa, come back to me, darlin'."

Darlin'? Who called her darlin'?

She blinked, desperate to see the man. His tone sounded worried. Tender. Almost loving.

She wanted to be loved so badly. Her mother hadn't loved her enough to stick around. And then her daddy hadn't, either...

A warm hand brushed her cheek. Masculine fingers. A touch that made her struggle harder, drawing her back toward the light.

"Melissa, darlin', you're going to be okay. The paramedics are here."

Paramedics?

She must be hurt. Was she in an accident?

Memories tugged at her mind. What had happened?

She'd come home, she was asleep. Was dreaming. Then the noise. Someone breaking in.

Her heart jumped to her throat, and she trembled.

"Shh, I've got you."

The male voice, so soothing. Comforting. Then big arms pulled her up against a broad chest. Hard but safe.

She blinked, determined to see his face. To tell him not to leave. That she liked his arms around her and his voice in her ear.

More voices. Footsteps. A door shutting. The man's arms slipped away.

She cried out for him not to leave. She was scared, although she didn't know of what. Dying?

Or of the man who'd broken in? Yes, a man. He'd grabbed her, thrown her against the wall. He aimed the rifle at her.

He was going to shoot her.

She screamed, her body jerking as she opened her eyes.

The gun was gone. The man was, too.

Dex was holding her, whispering her name. A tear slid down her cheek. "Don't leave me," she managed in a raspy whisper.

"I won't," he said in a husky voice. "I'll be right beside you."

But he released her, and two men lifted her onto a stretcher. She closed her eyes, the darkness drowning out the light again.

DEX BREATHED A sigh of relief that Melissa's vitals were stable. She might have a slight concussion and needed a couple of stitches on her forehead at her hairline, but she would be all right.

He'd been so damn grateful when she'd opened her eyes and looked at him that he'd nearly cried like a baby.

A sarcastic chuckle rumbled inside him. Lamar would have liked that. He'd always teased Dex about women, said when Dex fell, he'd fall hard.

Dex had laughed and blown off the comment. He'd insisted that would never happen to him.

But Lamar might be right. Melissa might be the one to do him in.

"I'll be right behind you and meet you at the hospital," he whispered to her as the medics secured her in the ambulance and closed the door.

Lamar had been taking pictures of the crime scene and body. Dr. Hudson, the ME from Austin, arrived on the heels of the ambulance, and joined Lamar.

Dex studied the dead man. "Does he have ID?"

Lamar checked the man's pockets. "Nothing in the shirt pockets." He checked his jeans. "Nothing there, either."

"I didn't see a car outside," Dex said. "How the hell did the bastard get here?"

Lamar worked his mouth from side to side as if contemplating the question. "Probably parked on another street and snuck in on foot."

True. The alleys connected side streets and offered hiding places for all kinds of nefarious activities.

Dex scanned the hallway and space around the body. "Did you find a phone?"

Lamar patted the man's clothing, then lifted the body slightly to check beneath him. A shake of his head indicated no phone, either.

Who the hell traveled without ID these days? Maybe another homeless person? But why attack Melissa?

"No drugs on him, either, but he could have been looking for cash or valuables to steal and sell," Lamar suggested.

That was a possibility, especially in Melissa's neighborhood. But why did he sense the break-in was connected to the case he was working?

Dex glanced at the ME. "Doc, what killed the bastard in the hospital?"

Dr. Hudson's brows furrowed. "He was just transported to the morgue. I haven't had time to perform the autopsy yet."

The poor doc must be working overtime these days.

The ME knelt by the dead man, speaking low into a mic attached to a recorder as he examined the body.

Dex was still trying to piece together what had happened tonight. "Melissa was unconscious when you arrived, Lamar?"

"Yeah, I told you that. The intruder turned the rifle on me. I had no choice but to shoot him."

Lamar snapped a picture of the rifle. "This belong to your friend?"

Dex shook his head. "I gave it to her for protection."

"Good God, Dex. You know people who aren't experienced with guns often get killed by having the weapon turned against them."

Dex nodded. But the thought of Melissa being unarmed seemed even more dangerous. "Look where she lives, man. She's nearly been killed twice this week. She needed protection."

Lamar shook his head as if he still didn't approve.

"What about him?" Dex asked. "Was he armed?"

Lamar lifted a bag containing a hunter's knife. An

image of the man holding that to Melissa's throat sent a chill through him. The jerk could have slit her throat in seconds.

Dr. Hudson rolled the body to the side and shined a small flashlight on his back. "One bullet to the chest. No exit wound. Bled out."

Lamar indicated his service revolver. "My weapon. The bullet will match. It'll all be in the report."

A knock sounded at the door, and one of the crime workers poked his head in. "Sergeant Eames and Officer Rafferty reporting."

Lamar met them at the door and explained the scene. The investigators booted up and entered. Officer Rafferty headed to the bedrooms to search for evidence, although judging from the broken glass in the window, the man had entered through the back doorway and Melissa had met him in the hallway. Scuff marks and blood marred the floor and walls leading toward the living room, but the fight had ended in the hallway.

"I'm going to the hospital to check on Melissa," Dex said.

He didn't want her to wake up and be alone.

Maybe the guy who'd attacked her had said something before he'd knocked her out. Something that would reveal his motive.

And if he was working for someone, maybe he'd given her a name.

MELISSA SLOWLY MADE her way back to reality. The doctor at the ER examined her and stitched her head. Two stitches. It wouldn't leave much of a scar.

Not that she cared that much about a little scar. She'd almost died.

She gripped the sheet as the nurse left the room. A second later, Dex walked in, his face a mask of anger. But his look softened as he approached her.

"Melissa?"

"I'm okay," she said softly. "I just want to get out of here."

"The doctor said you might have a concussion. You should stay the night for observation."

Tears filled her eyes. She hated hospitals, had seen too many sad stories of people from shelters who went in and never came out. "Please just take me home."

A muscle ticked in his jaw. "You're not going back to your house tonight. If the doctor releases you, I'll take you to Hawk's Landing."

Melissa had heard about the ranch from Dexter years ago. And then the stories in the press. She'd even seen pictures Dex had shown her. It was a beautiful place.

And his mother had turned it into a refuge for girls in trouble.

Dex traced a finger along her hand, his breathing ragged. "I know you probably don't want to talk about it right now. But I need you to tell me what happened tonight."

Emotions crowded her chest as memories of the night returned.

"This man, he broke in," she said in a low whisper. "What happened to him?"

"Lamar shot him. He said he found him with my rifle aimed at you." His voice cracked. "He saved your life, Melissa."

So now she was beholden to the detective.

But images of the man threatening to kill her returned. Then the look in his eyes when she'd pleaded for her life.

For a moment, she'd thought he intended to put down the gun. Leave her alone. Run.

But then…the siren. And he'd hit her and she'd blacked out.

After that, she had no idea what had happened.

Dex leaned forward, his thumb brushing the bandage where the doctor had stitched her up. "Did he say anything before he knocked you unconscious? Was he looking for money? Drugs?"

"No," she whispered. "I offered him money, but he told me to be quiet. I tried to persuade him to let me help him. Then the siren wailed and he…maybe he panicked. That's when he hit me."

Dex's gaze locked with hers. "I'm sorry. I should have been with you."

"It wasn't your fault, Dex."

"Maybe it was. I'm the one asking questions. If I hadn't been hauling you all over the place with me, you'd be safe."

She hated the guilt in Dex's voice. He didn't deserve that.

She reached for his hand, determined to reassure him. "Please get me out of here. Then we can talk."

She'd do everything possible to convince him that he had nothing to feel guilty about.

When she'd been on the brink of death, thinking of him had given her a reason to live.

Chapter Sixteen

Melissa's head throbbed as Dex drove, but she was so grateful to be leaving the hospital that she dared not complain, or Dex would have her admitted. Still, she closed her eyes and rested, although it was difficult to rest with the attack still fresh in her mind.

A half hour later, Dex passed under a sign for Hawk's Landing. She studied the property through the window. Moonlight glinted off the fields and pastures, the acres rolling out in an endless sea of green.

"This is beautiful," she murmured. "I can't imagine growing up with all this open space."

"It was pretty amazing," Dex said. "Until Chrissy disappeared."

That terrible event had marked his life.

He gestured toward a big farmhouse. "That's the main house where Mom lives with the foster girls."

"It's lovely," she said. "It looks homey."

"Mom has made it that way." Dex pointed out the horse stables, barns and cabins on the property. "Harrison and Honey live in that one," he said. "Honey helped design their house. She also worked with Charlotte and Lucas to design theirs and recently helped Brayden and his wife, Mila, build."

"I read about the project Honey undertook in Tumbleweed. She sounds amazing."

Dex nodded. "You know she grew up with nothing, though. Had a bad childhood. Her father was known as the town drunk."

Melissa's gaze locked with his. "Are you implying that we'd have something in common?"

A small smile tugged at the corner of his lips. "I think you'd like her. And Charlotte. She runs an art therapy program for troubled girls."

"I read about that when her studio was attacked." Melissa shivered. "Did you help your brother shut down that trafficking ring?"

"All my brothers and I had a hand in it." Dex sighed. "It was rough seeing what those girls went through. But at least now they have a chance at a life."

Like she tried to give the men hope at Lend-A-Hand.

Dex parked in front of a log cabin that backed to a wooded area. A front porch held a porch swing, and a hitching post for horses was built to the side.

"I have a small apartment in Austin, but I thought you'd like it out here better. It's peaceful and away from the city."

"You have a place in Austin, too?"

He nodded. "Above my PI office. But it's pretty bare. Only one bedroom." He parked and cut the engine. "Anybody could track me down at my office. The ranch is more secure. Harrison installed that security gate and cameras when Mom decided to foster the girls."

Melissa unbuckled her seat belt, but her legs felt shaky as she slid from the SUV. Dex hurried around and took her arm.

"You can lean on me," he said, his voice gruff.

"Thanks. I do feel a little unsteady."

"The doc said to watch you tonight. If you feel sick, you have to tell me."

In spite of the throbbing inside her skull, she managed a weak smile. "I'm fine, Dex."

The sound of horses neighing echoed from the pasture nearby as they made it up the porch steps. A slight breeze stirred the trees, a welcome relief from the summer heat. Dex unlocked the door, and Melissa felt as if she'd come home.

A log cabin quilt hung on the wall over a dark leather couch with a crocheted afghan tossed across the matching leather chair by the stone fireplace. The living area and kitchen were one big room with a vaulted ceiling and exposed beams. Picture windows flanking the fireplace offered an expansive view of the ranch.

"This is stunning," she said softly.

"Thanks. It's home."

Something she'd never had. He'd seen her unpacked boxes, the suitcase perched in her room, ready to be packed up so she could leave at a moment's notice.

He escorted her down a short hall to a bedroom on the right. "I promised the doc I'd make sure you rested. The guest room has its own bath, so make yourself at home." He pointed out the linen closet. "Clean towels are on the shelf. I don't have many guests, but I think there's soap, too."

How many women had he brought here? She hadn't asked if he was involved with anyone.

Maybe she didn't want to know.

She suddenly realized that she was still wearing the scrubs they'd given her at the hospital. The paramedics had bagged her clothes to give the detective so he could log them into evidence.

She gestured to the scrubs. "Do you have a T-shirt I could sleep in?"

His gaze skated over her, and her skin tingled. She'd slept naked with him ten years ago. The thought of crawling in bed with him again made her body hum with desire.

But the pain in her head and the scent of blood from her attacker sobered her.

She wasn't here to make love to Dex.

He'd brought her here for protection because someone had tried to kill her.

Dex excused himself and returned a minute later with a dark gray T-shirt emblazoned with the name of the ranch on it.

"It'll probably swallow you whole," he said as he handed it to her.

Her fingers brushed his as she took it from him. "It's perfect. If you don't mind, I might rinse off in the shower."

"Of course. Do you want a drink, or some tea?"

"Better not have a drink on top of the painkiller they gave me. Maybe hot tea?"

"You got it."

The temptation to ask if she needed help tugged at him, but he bit back the words. Dammit, she'd been beaten by one man tonight. She didn't need him asking anything from her.

He went to make the tea while she disappeared into the bathroom. The shower water kicked on, and he forced his mind away from images of her naked and wet. Instead, he decided to work.

He booted up his computer and ran a search on Dr. Huckleberry. Glowing testimonials praised the doctor's reputation and care of his patients. Comments about an auction house and rancher named Vance Baxter also were interspersed.

Dex entered Baxter's name and the auction house and found comments about the rancher and his business. Nothing shady. And no complaints.

That struck him as odd. Every rancher or breeder dealt with dissatisfied or disgruntled people. Breeding and the cattle business were big money. Money not everyone had.

A prize bull's seed was coveted and worth a small fortune.

The teakettle whistled, and he stood and turned off the gas burner. He set a mug on the counter with a tea bag ready for Melissa, then returned to his desk. He tapped his fingers on his thigh, the mystery of the missing homeless men still bothering him. He searched for the name Harry Willis, but he didn't show up in the system. Harry didn't have a record. Or a driver's license. Or any property.

Not surprising.

Curious, he tapped into missing persons' reports and searched for anything about the homeless men.

His pulse hammered. There were more than he expected. Six in the last twelve months ranging from Austin to Amarillo to Fort Worth. That was on top of the three he'd already noted that were recent.

Jim Smith's face flashed back, and he ran a search on the name. Dozens of hits. It took him a good half hour to scroll through them all. None matched the Jim Smith he'd met.

Smith claimed he'd had amnesia for years. But he hadn't mentioned exactly when he'd been attacked.

Dex rubbed his hand over his chin. Six missing homeless men didn't seem like that many, he supposed. He decided to expand the search, going back five years. Twenty-two names appeared. Many from the same areas as the recent missing men.

It would take time to review all these reports.

The bedroom door opened, and he closed his laptop for the night.

Melissa appeared in the doorway, looking small and vulnerable with her bruised face and those damn stitches. She also looked sexy as hell in his shirt.

He wanted to rip it off and make love to her.

But feeding his needs would be wrong.

So he walked to the counter, poured hot water into the mug, then dunked the tea bag into the cup. "You still take sugar?"

"You remembered?"

He nodded. There were so many things he remembered about her. One of them was how her voice had sounded purring his name when he was inside her.

Their gazes locked, and heat rippled between them.

For a second, he was afraid to move. Afraid he'd lose control and kiss her.

"You need to go to bed," he said instead. "The doc ordered you to rest."

Her face paled. "I know. But I'm not sure I can sleep."

He didn't think he could sleep, either.

"Come on, I'll tuck you in."

She laughed softly. He took her hand and walked her to the bedroom, then set the tea on the nightstand and turned down the covers.

She ran a hand through her damp hair, then looked up at him with such longing in her eyes that his body hardened.

Then she lifted her hand and pressed it against his cheek. His breath caught, the ache in his chest stirring full force.

Her eyes darkened. She released a sigh that echoed with need. Heat rose between them, and she pulled his face toward her, parted her lips and closed her mouth over his.

MELISSA HAD NO idea what had come over her. She never made the first move with a man. But she'd seen the hunger in Dex's eyes, and had remembered thinking she was going to die, and couldn't resist.

She didn't want to be alone tonight. She wanted Dex's lips and hands on her, to feel the beating of his heart beneath her hand and the whisper of his breath against her neck as he lay entwined with her.

She deepened the kiss, drawing his face closer to her, and he slid his fingers into her hair just the way he used to do. Need and desire bolted through her, and she ran her hands down his back, raking fingers over corded muscles that stirred her arousal even more.

He made a low sound in his throat, then teased her lips apart with his tongue and deepened the kiss. Their tongues mated and danced in a sensual rhythm that seemed so perfect it was as if they were made for one another.

He stroked her back and wrapped his arms around

her, their bodies brushing together. She reached for the buttons on his shirt, desperate to rake her fingers across his bare chest.

But he curled his fingers around her hand and stopped her, then leaned his head against hers. Their ragged breathing echoed in the charged silence.

Insecurity seized her. "Why did you stop? Is there someone else?"

"No," he said in a raw whisper. "But you just came from the hospital, Melissa. I'm not about to make love to you when you may have a concussion."

"I feel okay," she said, although the throbbing in her temple was growing more intense.

He chuckled. "You feel more than okay to me, but you need rest. And that's what you're going to get."

She wanted to pout, but he sounded so sweet and worried that emotions threatened to send her into a crying jag.

Afraid her feelings for him were written on her face, she averted her eyes and tugged the covers over her. He tucked her in as if she was a child. It was such a protective, loving gesture, one she'd never had from her parents, that a tear slid down her cheek.

"Ahh, Melissa. Are you in pain?"

She shook her head and traced a finger along his jaw. "Stay with me for a while, Dex."

He brushed her hair away from her cheek, the sexual heat returning. A myriad of emotions brimmed in his eyes, too. Ones she didn't understand. Ones she refrained from asking about.

Because she feared the answer.

That he'd tell her he could give her one night of loving. Then he'd walk away like he had before.

She didn't want to hear that right now.

But he didn't speak. He stretched out on top of the covers and pulled her into his arms. She snuggled against him, one hand on his chest so she could feel the heat of his body and the beating of his heart.

Hers belonged to him.

It terrified her. But she realized now that it always had.

HE WAS IN TROUBLE. Deep trouble.

Melissa Gentry was boring a hole in his hardened heart and climbing in.

He slowly stroked her hair, willing himself to stay strong and keep his hands off her, which was damn near impossible.

Finally she drifted to sleep. The bruises on her face and her neck looked darker tonight. Stark against the moonlight shimmering through the window.

Fury railed inside him at the fact that someone had physically hurt her.

She sighed in her sleep, her breathing growing steady. Thank God she'd survived.

He needed to watch her. Wake her a couple of times and make sure she didn't have a serious head injury.

Although she'd looked at him with such desire that he'd almost forgotten about the case and why he'd brought her here.

He couldn't forget. Protecting her was his job at the moment. When he figured out what was going on, though, they'd part ways. They'd have to.

He could not lose himself in a woman.

You already have, buddy.

Body wound tight with anxiety, he eased her hand from his chest. Dammit, he missed her sweet touch.

But he didn't deserve her.

He eased off the bed, gently settling her head against the pillow and making sure she was covered. Then he tiptoed from the room.

He needed to work. Too late to call Lucas, though. Besides, Charlotte was due any day now. She needed him.

Still, he texted him about the business card and prints and told him that he'd leave the card in an envelope on the table by the door so Lucas could swing by, pick it up and carry it to the lab.

Unable to sleep, he walked into the kitchen for a drink.

But as he bypassed the arrowhead collection on the wall by the door, nostalgia hit him. Memories of him and Chrissy hunting for the arrowheads. They'd made up stories about how the arrowheads ended up on Hawk's Landing.

A noise echoed from the bedroom, and he hurried to check on Melissa. She was still sleeping, but had rolled to her side.

The need to hold her seized him, but he returned to the den.

He slid in front of his laptop, booted it up and checked hospitals and morgues for Harry Willis. Nothing popped.

Then he decided to search records of missing homeless men that had been reported, this time dating back fifteen years.

His pulse jumped. Several more names appeared.

Two that were close to Tumbleweed. Two that occurred around the time his sister went missing.

Sheriff Dunar, the sheriff who'd investigated his sister's disappearance and then his father's, had been notified of the missing men.

He studied the names, then poured himself a beer and went outside to think. Tomorrow he'd talk to the former sheriff and see what he'd learned about the men.

If someone had been preying on the homeless eighteen years ago and had continued all these years, they were dealing with a serial predator.

It was time to stop him before he killed again.

Chapter Seventeen

Dex checked on Melissa several more times during the night. Satisfied she was all right, he finally snatched a couple of hours of sleep himself, then rose and made coffee. He carried his mug to the porch to watch the horses run and to keep himself from crawling in bed with her.

He had to focus. Today he'd talk to that rancher, and Sheriff Dunar.

God, his father had loved this land. Had worked hard to build the ranch. He'd also seemed like such a family man. Granted, he'd worked him and his brothers, and he'd sure as hell disciplined them, but he'd used a gentle hand.

Finding out Chrissy wasn't his father's birth child had been a shocker to him and his brothers. But apparently his father had known years ago, had forgiven his mother, and had loved Chrissy as if she was his own.

Those damn arrowheads were nagging at him. Smith had talked about a rock formation—

"Dex?"

Melissa's voice jolted him from his thoughts. Morning sunlight dappled her beautiful face and cast subtle red streaks in her dark hair.

He wanted to run his fingers through it again.

Oh, yeah, he had it bad.

"There's coffee," he said.

She stepped onto the porch and offered him a smile, gesturing to the mug in her hand. "Thanks. I found it."

She still wore his damn T-shirt, which came to her knees and looked like a dress on her. He wondered if she had underwear beneath it.

She eased into the rocking chair beside him and pushed it with her feet, her gaze traveling across the pasture. A black stallion galloped on the hill, its mane flying in the wind as it ran.

For a moment, they settled into a peaceful lull where he imagined waking up with her like this every day. Sharing morning coffee together on the porch after a long night of lovemaking. Then they'd saddle up and go for a ride to the creek...

And one day there'd be a kid running around in the yard. A little boy. Or maybe a girl. It didn't matter. He'd teach him or her to ride, and they'd go to his favorite fishing spot and then picnic by the pond.

He bolted up from the chair. Good God, what had gotten into him? He'd planned to stay single forever. Had never wanted to be a family man because it hurt too damn much when that family fell apart.

"Dex?" Her voice sounded worried.

"I'll fix us some breakfast."

"I'll help."

"No," he said more brusquely than he'd intended. The last thing he needed was Melissa in his kitchen, planting memories of the two of them cooking their morning meal together. That seemed even more intimate than sharing a bed.

"Last night I did some research after you fell asleep. There have been several more reports of missing homeless men the past eighteen years. I'm going to talk to the former sheriff about them."

She stood. "Okay. If you drive me home, I'll change and go with you."

"No, I should do this alone." He gazed back at the pasture, anything to distract himself from her. "Besides, the cleanup crew is scheduled to come to the shelter. I'll drive you there to meet them."

She agreed, and he left her on the porch to enjoy her coffee while he scrambled some eggs. He needed some distance between them today to get his head straight. She wouldn't be safe until he solved this case.

And he'd never walk away from her while she was still in danger.

MELISSA LIKED WAKING up and having coffee with Dex. Maybe too much. She yearned to do it every day.

He obviously didn't feel the same way. He'd almost looked panicked when she'd joined him, then he'd bolted inside as quickly as he could.

She blinked away tears. This nasty headache and the trauma of being shot at and attacked were making her weepy and…weak.

She couldn't fall into the trap of believing a relationship with Dex would last. It hadn't before. And he hadn't changed.

Had he?

She swallowed disappointment as the answer screamed in her head.

She breathed in the fresh air and scent of grass and wildflowers, and finished her coffee. Today she'd get the shelter back in shape. Then she could start back to work.

Work was exactly what she needed. Focusing on helping others distracted her from silly dreams that would never come true.

Dex poked his head out. "Breakfast is ready."

"Thanks." She stepped inside and joined him at the table, although an awkward silence fell between them. As soon as they finished, he cleared the table, and she hurried to dress. The scrubs were a stark reminder of what had happened the day before.

In the car, she texted April to inform her about the cleanup crew, then they stopped at her house. The sight of fingerprint dust and blood made her pause as she entered, and a shudder coursed through her as she relived the break-in.

"You okay?" Dex asked in a gruff voice.

She squared her shoulders, determined not to fall apart. "I need to clean in here, too."

"When the crew finishes at the shelter, they can come here."

She valued her independence, but she wasn't a fool, either, so she agreed. She didn't want a repeat of the night before. It might not end with minor injuries this time.

She hurried into the bedroom, stripped the scrubs and dressed in jeans and a T-shirt. A quick exam in the mirror, and she winced at the dark circles beneath her eyes and the bruises on her forehead and neck.

No wonder Dex had avoided her this morning. She looked as if she'd been run over by a truck.

Reminding herself it didn't matter, she grabbed her

purse and joined him in the hall where he was waiting. He was studying the place where her attacker had died.

"Something wrong?" she asked.

"I don't know. Lamar shot your attacker in the chest. I was just thinking that from where you were lying, if the intruder was facing you, when Lamar rushed in, he would have been behind the bastard." He made a sound of frustration. "Lamar must have identified himself, and the guy swung around to face him, then Lamar shot him."

"That makes sense," Melissa said.

Dex nodded, although he remained quiet as they drove to the shelter. When they arrived, he scanned the property and walked her to the door. The cleanup crew hadn't yet shown up, but they went inside. Dex hurried to the bunk room to see if Smith was hiding inside.

But he was gone.

"WHERE DO YOU think Smith would go?" Dex asked.

"I don't know. He's scared." Melissa sighed. "Even without a threat, it's hard for these drifters to stay put. Moving has become a way of life. It's easier than getting attached and having to say goodbye."

His eyes darkened. "Is that the way you feel?"

She shrugged. "Moving is all I've ever known."

Another reason he needed to maintain his control. He'd had too many people walk out on him to chance it again. He'd seen that suitcase waiting and ready.

Hell, after this was over, he couldn't blame her if she did want to move.

The crime scene cleanup crew arrived, and he showed them in, then explained about Melissa's house.

He didn't want to leave her alone, but at least people were here, and it was early morning, so she should be safe.

"I'm fine, Dex. I have some work to do in my office anyway."

"Call me if you need me."

Their gazes locked again, heat and emotions simmering between them.

"I'll be back in a little while." She nodded, and he left and drove to the former sheriff's cabin on the lake.

Harrison had been elected as sheriff when Sheriff Dunar retired. He and his wife had settled into a peaceful retreat in the woods on the river.

Sheriff Dunar's graying hair was patchy, his face thin and drawn. Although his belly suggested he probably enjoyed a beer or two while fishing.

"This is funny," Sheriff Dunar said. "Just saw your brother Harrison a few months ago. And now you're here." He shoved a fishing hat on his head. "I was sorry about your daddy."

Dex swallowed. "Yeah. Thanks."

"Is that why you're here? 'Cause I thought he had an accident."

"He did." Dex explained about the shooting at the shelter and his theories regarding the missing homeless men. "A couple of homeless men also went missing near Tumbleweed around the time Chrissy disappeared. Do you remember those reports?"

Dunar stared out at the woods. "Yeah. Homeless Joe and Creepy Karl," Dunar said. "Never found either of them, but Joe was a roamer. He'd been sleeping on the streets for years. Took odd jobs at different ranches for a while when he was younger. But after he had an accident with a bull, he landed near Tumbleweed."

"You knew him?" Dex asked.

Dunar shrugged. "I saw him around town a few times. Seemed harmless. Think he and Honey Granger's daddy were drinking buddies."

"Who reported him missing?" Dex asked.

"Ethel Wiggins from the Baptist church. She volunteered carrying meals to the needy."

"I'd like to talk to her," Dex said.

"Afraid that's not possible," the sheriff said. "She passed about five years ago."

Dammit. "And Karl? Why did they call him Creepy?"

"He was touched in the head," Dunar said. "Used to string arrowheads together and wear 'em around his neck, then talked to himself all the time. Nothing coherent."

Dex frowned. He and Chrissy had found dozens of arrowheads on Hawk's Landing.

There were arrowheads all over Texas, though. Didn't mean Karl had found any on the ranch.

He folded his hands, thinking. "The report on Chrissy's disappearance indicated that a homeless man was a person of interest."

Sheriff Dunar's bushy brows bunched into a unibrow. "Yeah, but that old man died of liver failure."

A dead end there. Unless someone had killed him and covered it up.

"Are you sure?" Dex asked.

The sheriff folded his arms. "That's what the ME said. Why are you asking about these men? They were drifters. They moved around all the time. And to tell you the truth, once your sister and then your daddy disappeared, they took priority."

Dex had mixed feelings about that. Selfishly he

wanted his family to take priority, but…the sheriff shouldn't have ignored these reports, either. "I think someone has been preying on homeless men, and that they've been doing it for nearly two decades and have gotten away with it."

Shock streaked the sheriff's eyes. "What? That's crazy."

Dex shook his head. "Maybe not." It was possible that his father had been one of the victims. Someone could have poured that alcohol down his throat.

He needed to talk to the ME who'd autopsied his father. Make sure there weren't injuries that could have caused him to crash other than alcohol. The booze could have been the killer's way of covering up his crime.

A dark thought crept into his head. His father, the missing homeless men…if he was right, the crimes had begun on this man's watch. Sheriff Dunar had been the only law enforcement eighteen years ago.

What if he'd known what was going on and had kept the truth hidden all these years?

MELISSA AND APRIL spent the morning in the office while the crime scene crew cleaned up the common area in the shelter. April notified the other agencies to inform them that they were open again.

"The volunteer at Another Chance said they haven't seen Gunther in over twenty-four hours," April said.

"Do they have any idea where he went?"

April shook her head. "He said he'd found some work, and that he was going to take it."

That could be a good thing. "What kind of work?"

"He wouldn't say. She heard him talking about cattle

to one of the other men, so maybe he'd gotten a job as a ranch hand. But when she asked him, he clammed up."

Melissa rubbed her temple. Her headache was returning in full force. She hoped Gunther had found work and was trying to get back on his feet. But considering what had happened the last few days and Dex's suspicions, worry gnawed at her.

The crime scene cleanup crew finished, and Melissa gave them her home address. "I'll meet you there."

"Mr. Hawk is sending a repairman to fix your broken window."

Yes, that needed to be done.

She thanked them, then left April to finish ordering supplies and straightening the bunk room. Outside, she phoned a cab to drive her home. But a noise from the alley startled her, and she jerked her head around.

A low moan reverberated from behind a trash can. Heart racing, she inched toward the alley.

Another moan. The trash can rattled. Then a bloody hand reached around the side of it and clawed at the ground.

Chapter Eighteen

Fear seized Melissa at the sight of the bloody hand reaching toward her from the back of the trash can. Could be a drug dealer or victim of a crime. Or…Jim Smith. God, maybe someone had killed him and left him in the alley.

She pulled her phone from her pocket, but a voice called for help, and she rushed forward. She couldn't see the man, but blood covered his fingers, and bloody prints marked the wall behind the dumpster.

She inched closer, scanning the area for trouble. Footsteps pounded the pavement down the alley. Pulse hammering, she veered around the edge of the dumpster.

"Help me…" the voice rasped.

A man in ragged jeans and a bloody plaid shirt lay facedown as he tried to crawl away from the wall. Emotions clogged her throat as he heaved for a breath.

Gently she caught his arm and rolled him to his side. Not a stranger or Smith. Gunther.

His face was ghost white, his eyes bloodshot and wide-eyed, his mouth gaping open as he struggled to draw a breath. Blood soaked his chest and both his hands, and pooled beneath his body. A drop of blood seeped from his nose.

She sat down on the ground beside him and pulled his head into her lap, soothing him with gentle strokes along his cheek. With her other hand she dialed 9-1-1. "Send an ambulance. Hurry, a man is hurt badly!" She gave the operator the address, praying Gunther made it.

His body jerked and convulsed, then he spit blood as he tried to speak.

"I'm here, Gunther," she murmured. "Hang in there, help is on the way."

He gasped, choking on garbled words. His bloody hand rose to claw at her arm, but he was so weak it fell to his side, and a moan rumbled from him.

"Please, Gunther, hang in there. You have to tell me who did this so I can make him pay."

Another gasp. A siren wailed close by. Coming closer. The ambulance would be there soon. More noise down the street. Voices. Arguing. Someone running. What was going on?

She scanned the street, praying whoever had hurt Gunther wasn't still lurking around.

The bloody hand clawed at her arm, urging her closer. He was going to tell her who'd done this.

She leaned closer, but his ragged breath puffed out. His eyelids flickered closed, then open, then his eyes rolled back in his head.

Panic made tears burn her eyes. "Gunther, please, hang in there," Melissa whispered.

The siren wailed again. Louder. Tires screeched. Lights twirled in the parking lot of the shelter.

She rocked Gunther in her arms, begging him to

stay alive. But another breath rasped out, and it turned out to be his last. He died in her arms.

DEX PHONED BAXTER to verify that he was home before he made the long drive to the man's ranch. The housekeeper informed him that Baxter was at the auction house, so Dex headed that direction first.

He'd done his research this morning before Melissa had woken up. Vance Baxter had inherited his land from his father when Vance was only eighteen. Vance's father died of a heart attack while driving his herd from one pasture to the next, and had collapsed right on their land.

According to his research, Vance's mother fell ill and died a year after she lost her husband. Just as it had in his own family, the ranch went downhill after that.

Four years after Vance's father's death, the property was about to go into foreclosure. But Vance had taken business classes by then, and he managed to sell off a portion of land he wasn't using to have cash to work with. Then he hired Emmet Wilson, to help him fine-tune his stock. Wilson's techniques had garnered Vance a prize stud. Selling the stud's sperm earned him enough profit to expand his herd, and his business took off. A couple of years later, he opened the auction house.

A large sign advertising the upcoming auction schedule hung in front of the auction house. Two trucks with trailers were parked to the side of the main building. A barn and pens for housing the cattle when they were transported here for auction day sat to the left while another building lay to the right.

Dex parked in front. The auction house looked simple and basic, but expensive deals were made in this facility. Vance Baxter had gone from nearly losing his family ranch to accumulating a small fortune. His business practices had earned him respect in the ranching community. If Vance's father had lived, he would have been proud.

Dex knew what it was like to lose your father.

Then Vance had lost his mother, too. Those losses could have crushed him, but they seemed to have driven him to success. It was difficult not to admire him because he was a self-made icon in the ranching community. Ranchers traveled from all over Texas and even from other states to purchase one of his studs.

Although Dex had heard that Vance could be ruthless in business. Maybe his success had gone to his head? Or had he made his fortune by taking advantage of others?

A man in overalls and a cowboy hat strode from the building and climbed in one of the trucks that was hitched to a trailer. His scowl made Dex wonder just what had transpired between him and Baxter. He was leaving with an empty trailer, too.

The sign out front indicated the next auction was at six that night.

Was the rancher returning for the auction?

A couple of workers exited another building to the left as Dex slid from his SUV. A blonde woman with big hair and heavy makeup greeted Dex as he entered the front door. Her ruby-red lips parted into a grin as her gaze skated over him.

"Hey there, cowboy, you here to register for the auction?"

Dex offered her a small smile. Melissa, with her

simple clothes and no makeup, was far more attractive than this dolled-up female. "No, I'd like to talk to Vance Baxter."

She checked the calendar. "Do you have an appointment?"

Dex shook his head. "No, but I think he'll see me. Just tell him Dexter Hawk from Hawk's Landing is here to talk to him. I'm interested in his services."

A lie would get him through the door faster than the truth.

The girl excused herself, then returned a minute later with Baxter behind her.

He was in his forties now, tall and lean with a goatee and silver streaking the hair at his temples. Although he was dressed in a Western shirt and jeans, he wore an expensive-looking gold watch and a gold signet ring with the logo for his business etched on it.

"Thank you for seeing me." Dex extended his hand and Baxter shook it. "Dexter Hawk."

Baxter gave a slight nod of recognition. "I met one of your brothers a while back. You own Hawk's Landing, right?"

Dex nodded. "Sure do. We've been hearing about your success for a while now."

The man grinned. "Thanks. Come on back." Baxter motioned for him to follow, and Dex walked behind him through a set of doors, then down a narrow hall to a massive office on the right. Sleek cherrywood furniture mixed with metal bookshelves gave the place a rustic yet classy feel.

Photographs on the wall showcased Baxter accepting numerous awards for his breeding and included pictures of satisfied customers and their purchases—

a testimonial for his business obviously meant to impress potential customers and buyers.

"So, Mr. Hawk, my receptionist said you're interested in my services. I thought you and your brothers were focusing on the equine business."

Dex offered a small nod, surprised that Baxter knew that much about him and Hawk's Landing. "Yes, at this point we are. But we're open to expansion. You're familiar with our ranch?"

"You and your family have been in the news a lot lately."

Dex grimaced at that comment.

"I was sorry to hear about your daddy," Vance said, his voice sincere. "A shame after all these years that it turned out that way."

"Yes, it was," Dex said. More than a shame. "You have an impressive operation. Congratulations on your success."

"Staying relevant is key," Vance said. "I try to keep up with the latest science and breeding techniques. So far, it's worked." He lifted a brochure from a stack on his desk and pushed it toward Dex. His chest puffed up with pride as he described his connection with Emmet Wilson.

"If you're interested in expanding the cattle side of your operation, I'm holding an auction tonight. Six o'clock."

"Maybe next time. I'll certainly discuss it with my brothers," Dex said.

Baxter leaned back in his chair and folded his arms, scrutinizing Dex. "So, why are you really here, Mr. Hawk?"

Dex forced himself not to react, although he'd been

scanning the room and the man's desk, and he noticed a business card tucked beneath the brochures. The logo and name looked familiar.

The PI, Clark McTruitt.

"If you've followed the news, I suppose you've seen the story about the woman at the Lend-A-Hand homeless shelter being attacked."

Vance's eyes narrowed. "Yes."

"The man who broke in was a private investigator, Clark McTruitt. Did you know him?"

Vance averted his gaze. "Afraid not."

Dex raised a brow. "Really? That looks like his card on your desk."

Baxter gave a shrug. "He could have stopped in a while back. To tell you the truth, I deal with so many people, I forget."

Yeah, right. "So you didn't hire him?"

"Hire him?" Baxter grunted. "Why would I need a PI?"

"I don't know, that's why I'm asking," Dex said.

Baxter straightened, running his fingers over his bolo tie. "Why do I sense you're interrogating me now? What is this really about?"

Dex maintained a neutral expression, although the air in the room became charged with resentment. "McTruitt broke in looking for a homeless man named Jim Smith."

Baxter flattened his hands on his desk. "Again, what does that have to do with me?"

"Smith claims he has amnesia, said he was attacked years ago. He remembers coming to this auction house."

Baxter averted his gaze. "I don't know anyone named

Jim Smith. That said, my auctions draw hundreds of people at any one event, so I can't possibly know every one of them."

Baxter knew more than he'd admitted. Dex had to push a little harder. He removed his phone, then showed Baxter a picture of his dead father. "I think my father was homeless before he died. I've also discovered there are more than a dozen homeless men who've disappeared over the past two decades across Texas. Two disappeared around the time my father did eighteen years ago."

Baxter frowned. "What exactly are you implying, Mr. Hawk?"

"I think someone is preying on homeless men." He listed the names of the most recent missing men. "I also think someone hired McTruitt to kill Smith before he could remember what happened when he was attacked."

A calm rage seethed in Baxter's gray eyes. "I wish I could help you, but I can't. Now, it's time you left. I have business to attend to."

"Don't you think it's strange that the vet you work with was murdered?"

Shock bolted across Baxter's face. "Murdered? I thought one of the bulls attacked him."

Dex shook his head. "Whoever killed him put him in that stall so it would appear accidental."

Another tense second passed. "That's horrible. I certainly hope they find out who did that. But I can assure you his death has nothing to do with me." Baxter dropped all pretense of being nice. "I don't appreciate you coming here under the guise of wanting to work with me, Mr. Hawk. If you need to talk to me again, go through my attorney."

Of course he'd lawyer up. That only made him look guilty to Dex.

"Understood, but if you know anything about Dr. Huckleberry's death, or McTruitt, or these missing homeless men, then you need to speak up or you could be considered an accomplice to murder."

Baxter shot up from his seat and gestured toward the door. "Get out."

Dex simply smiled and thanked him, then stepped into the hallway.

His cell phone buzzed just as he passed the receptionist. Her wary gaze indicated she'd overheard their conversation.

His phone buzzed again as he stepped outside, and he checked the number. The ME from Tumbleweed. He quickly connected. "Dexter Hawk."

"It's Dr. Weinberger. You asked me to review your father's autopsy report."

"Yeah. Did you find anything?"

"As a matter of fact, I did. The tox screen was definitely positive, but there was a serious contusion on the back of your father's head that wasn't consistent with the accident. It cracked his skull."

Dex froze by his vehicle. "The back of his head. He hit facedown on the steering wheel."

"Exactly."

"Then it's possible that that blow to the head could have killed him?"

"Yes, it's possible."

Dex's pulse pounded. If it had, then it meant his father's death wasn't a DUI accident.

He was murdered.

Chapter Nineteen

The realization that his father had been murdered
echoed in Dex's ears. "Is there anything else you can
tell me?"

"Yes. With this much alcohol in the man's system, it
suggested he was an alcoholic, but there was no signs
of liver disease in the autopsy. In fact, his liver was in
great shape."

Dex contemplated that information. "So it's possible that someone forced the whiskey down his throat,
then killed him and staged his death as an accident?"

"I can't say with all certainty, but it's possible."

Dex's pulse hammered. Why would someone have
killed his father? Was his murder related to the other
missing homeless men?

"I'm sorry, Dex, I understand you and your family
have been through a lot."

"Thanks, I appreciate your help," Dex said gruffly.
"What we want now is the truth."

He ended the call, then dialed Lucas as he got in his
SUV and started the engine. Lucas sounded slightly
harried as he answered.

"Everything okay?" Dex asked.

"Yeah, but Charlotte was having some contractions. Turned out to be a false alarm. Braxton-Hicks. We just got back from the hospital. But I did pick up that card and dropped it off to have the prints analyzed."

"Thanks, Lucas." He paused, then pushed on. "I asked Dr. Weinberger to review Dad's autopsy."

Lucas sighed. "And?"

Dex relayed his conversation with the ME. "You'll probably think this is a long shot, but there were two other homeless men who disappeared around the time Chrissy and Dad did. I think it's all connected. That Dad was murdered because he knew something about it."

A long pause. "All right, we'll look into it. I'll compile a board with all the facts you've uncovered so far and persons of interest. Send me anything else you've dug up."

His phone was buzzing with another call. Melissa. Dammit, what if something was wrong?

"Melissa's calling, Lucas. Let me make sure she's all right."

They agreed to meet to review the information they'd gathered and pool their mental resources, then he quickly connected to Melissa.

A ragged breath echoed over the line, making nerves coil inside his belly.

"Melissa? Are you all right?"

Another second passed, then a low cry. Fear stole his breath.

"Talk to me, darlin'. What's wrong?"

"It's Gunther…" she said in a raw whisper. "I found him…dead…outside the shelter."

Dexter pressed the accelerator and swung onto the highway. "Hang on. I'm on my way."

Terror for Melissa choked him as he sped toward the shelter.

April joined Melissa outside the shelter while they waited on the ambulance and police.

"Poor Gunther," April said with tears in her eyes. "The volunteer at Another Chance said he was excited about that work. And now…he'll never have a chance to get his life back together."

"I know, it's not fair," Melissa said.

"Do you think he was attacked by a thief or gang?" April asked.

"Dex thinks the other missing men are connected to Jim Smith." Melissa hesitated. "Maybe Jim Smith uncovered what was going on with them, and someone tried to kill him to cover it up."

The ambulance rolled up, a police car on its tail. Medics jumped out and rushed toward her, and Detective Lamar exited his vehicle and followed. "What happened?"

"I came outside to catch a cab to go home, and I heard a noise in the alley." The image of that bloody hand reaching for help flashed behind her eyes. "Then I found Gunther bleeding and…gasping for breath."

The detective tugged his gun belt up on his hips. "You know the victim?"

Melissa nodded. "He stayed here at the shelter. He was…a good guy."

Melissa stepped away from Gunther. April hovered beside her, twisting her hands together.

A second later, the ME arrived and walked over to

them. One of the medics stood with a negative shake of his head indicating there was nothing they could do, then addressed the ME. "We'll transport him when you're ready."

Detective Lamar crossed to Gunther, pulled on gloves, then stooped down beside the ME who was conducting his own examination. Melissa strained to hear their conversation, but they spoke in hushed tones.

The detective snapped a few photos on his phone, then made a phone call before turning back to her. "A crime team is on the way. Ms. Gentry, did you hear anything or see anyone else when you came out here?"

"I heard voices farther down the alley. But I didn't recognize them or hear what they were saying." Melissa massaged her temple. "Then I thought I heard footsteps running."

"This is a busy part of town with bars nearby," the detective pointed out.

Melissa shifted. That was true.

The sound of tires screeching halted their conversation, and Dex sped into the parking lot, jumped out and jogged toward her.

Detective Lamar acknowledged him with a grunt. Concern darkened Dex's eyes. "Are you okay?"

She nodded. Emotions thickened her throat. "I found Gunther in the alley, but…he didn't make it."

Dex scanned the alley, then glanced at the body. "What was the cause of death?"

Detective Lamar jammed his hands on his hips. "Bled out from a gunshot wound to the chest. Close range."

"What caliber of gun?"

The detective pulled a baggie from his pocket and

dangled it. ".45. Bullet was a through and through. I'll log it into evidence and see if it matches any from another crime."

The ME strode toward them. "I'll do the autopsy as soon as possible. But I have a couple stacked up in front of him."

Detective Lamar turned to Melissa. "Do you know who his next of kin is?"

Melissa blinked back tears. So many of the homeless died alone with no one to mourn them or give them a proper burial. She hated for Gunther to be added to the list. "He didn't have any family."

"Then he'll be buried by the county," Detective Lamar said.

"No," Dex cut in. "I'll cover the cost of his funeral."

Melissa's heart melted at Dex's generosity. His thoughtfulness and respect for the people she tried to help moved her more than words.

He was such an honorable man.

No wonder she'd fallen for him ten years ago, and was falling for him again.

DEX STUDIED THE scene as the crime workers arrived and began to comb the alleys and trash cans for the murder weapon and forensic evidence.

He was damn glad to see that Melissa was all right. Upset, but at least she wasn't harmed.

She and April retreated inside the shelter to tie up plans so they could reopen, although he wondered if another murder so close to the shelter might make them rethink that decision. He sure as hell didn't want her anywhere near this place.

But telling Melissa that would only cause an argument. She was determined to help others at any cost to herself.

For God's sake, someone had to protect the damn woman.

A plan formed in his mind. He'd arrange for security cameras for the exterior of the premises to be installed. Simply having them in place would deter some criminals from approaching, and the cameras would help capture the goings-on around the shelter. Better security should have been put in place a long time ago.

But these facilities operated on government funds that were slim and didn't leave room for extras.

He had a little money put aside. He'd make it his mission to help if he could.

The ME walked over to where he stood by Lamar and addressed the detective. "When your crime techs finish with their pictures, you can have the body transported to the morgue. I'll be there working."

Detective Lamar nodded. "Shouldn't be long."

Dr. Hudson scowled at Dex. "I heard your ME in Tumbleweed pulled my report on your father."

Dex bit the inside of his cheek. "I did. And he told me something you failed to mention."

Dr. Hudson raised a brow. "I put everything in my report."

Detective Lamar glanced between the men. "What's this about, Dex?"

Dex spoke in a lethally calm voice. "Dr. Weinberger said my father had a cracked skull from a blow to the back of his head. That blow could have killed him, but you didn't mention it."

The ME squared his shoulders, chin jutted up in

challenge. "That injury looked old. I didn't find clear evidence to substantiate that it was COD."

"Then maybe you made a mistake," Dex suggested.

Irritation flared in the doctor's eyes. Detective Lamar stepped in. "Dex, don't start throwing stones. Considering the amount of alcohol in your father's bloodstream, and the trauma to the front of his head, Dr. Hudson's conclusions seem spot-on."

One of the crime techs motioned to Lamar, and he hurried over to the dumpster. Dex followed, curious. The male tech, who was knee-deep in the dumpster, lifted a bloody rag from the trash. "Looks like gunpowder residue on the rag. Maybe the killer wrapped it around the gun when he fired to drown out the noise."

Lamar handed the crime tech a bag, and the man slipped the rag inside. "Test it for GSR, prints and DNA. If we find a match, we can catch this guy."

Dex shifted. Maybe they'd finally gotten a lead. But if a serial predator had been killing homeless men for years, why would he be so sloppy to dump a rag with his DNA on it so near where he'd disposed of a body? And why leave this body in plain sight when so many others hadn't been recovered?

Because they aren't all connected. Some of them are just missing transients.

That was the logical answer. And it could be true—but at least *some* of them were related. Dex would bet his PI license on that.

The fact that someone had tried to kill him and Melissa proved they were on the right track.

Lamar angled his head toward Dex. "It's obvious you care about this woman. Why don't you take Melissa home and away from all this?"

"I need answers," Dex said. "Thinking my father died in a DUI accident is eating me up inside."

Lamar gripped his shoulder and gave it a squeeze. "I'm sorry for what your family has been through. Trust me, I'm here for you."

Lamar had rescued Dex when he was in trouble years ago, had mentored him and been a role model. Sure he'd skirted the line, but he never quite crossed it and was relentless in digging for the truth, always solving the case and making sure the victims received justice.

He had to trust his buddy. He wouldn't let him down. "Thanks. I think I will drive Melissa home. She deserves for someone to take care of her for a change."

Lamar's understanding expression indicated that Dex was in trouble where Melissa was concerned. Dex couldn't deny it, either.

He was drowning so deep in her sweetness, he didn't know if anyone could pull him out from under her spell.

Worse, he didn't know if he wanted to be pulled out.

"Are you sure we should reopen?" April asked. "Under the circumstances, I'm afraid letting people come here will endanger them."

Melissa couldn't shake the image of Gunther from her mind. "You're right. We should hold off. Will you let the other shelters know?"

"Of course." April hugged her. "Are you going to be okay tonight alone?"

"She won't be alone."

Dex's gruff voice sounded protective, almost territorial. April raised a questioning brow as he approached.

"I'll guard her tonight and make sure she's safe."

Melissa started to argue, but truthfully, she didn't want to be alone. She wanted Dex with her.

"Thanks, April. How about you? Will you be okay?"

April nodded. "I called my boyfriend. I'm going to his place for the night."

"Good." Melissa hugged her again, and then turned to Dexter.

"Come on," he said. "Let's go home."

"The crime cleanup team is at my house," Melissa said. "I was supposed to meet them."

"You aren't going there now." He removed his phone from his belt and sent a quick text. "They'll take care of things and lock up. Tomorrow we'll talk about installing security cameras at the shelter and your house."

She didn't argue with that, either. At this point, anything to ensure the safety of the men and volunteers at the shelter was important.

She and April agreed to talk later, and Dex walked her to his SUV. His jaw was set tight, the silence thick as they drove back to Hawk's Landing.

When they arrived at his cabin, he ushered her inside as if he thought someone might be on their tails.

Pain radiated from him as he faced her in the kitchen. Something had happened to upset him. Something he hadn't told her yet. "Dex? What's wrong?"

"The ME's report on my father. Dr. Weinberger says he suffered blunt force trauma to the back of his head."

"I don't understand," Melissa whispered. "You mean in the accident?"

"No. He hit face forward on the steering wheel." Dex pulled her to him, his voice a husky whisper. "I think he was murdered."

The agony in his voice tore at her heart, and she couldn't help herself. She loved him so much.

She pulled him into her arms and held him, soothing him as his body shook with emotions he didn't want her to see. A second later, he murmured her name, then closed his mouth over hers.

Chapter Twenty

Melissa deepened the kiss, tugging Dex so close she felt his hard chest against her breasts. He wrapped his arms around her and teased her lips apart with his tongue, his hands skating down to her hips. He drew her into the V of his thighs, and his hard length brushed her belly through his jeans.

Need rose inside her, memories of the times they'd been together in the past returning to taunt her. She knew his touch, his kiss, the way he felt inside her.

She wanted that feeling again.

He stroked her back, then brushed her hair aside with one hand and planted soft tender kisses along her throat. Erotic sensations splintered through her. Today had been tense, sad, painful.

She wanted Dex to erase that pain. And she wanted to ease his suffering.

He lifted his head suddenly, as if sensing her turmoil. His eyes searched hers. Anguish streaked his face. He'd just learned his father was murdered.

That was eating at him, resurrecting his grief and anger, which would drive him until he found his father's killer.

She tunneled her fingers through his hair, raking a

strand from his forehead. "I know you're hurting, Dex. I'm sorry about your father."

Regret flashed in his eyes. "And I'm sorry about Gunther."

Fresh tears blurred her eyes. She didn't know if she was crying for Gunther, or Dex, or because she was so in love with this strong man that she could barely breathe.

Intense emotions overcame her, and she kissed him again.

"Melissa," he murmured as she trailed her fingers down to unbutton his shirt.

"I need you, Dex," she whispered.

A low moan erupted from his throat, and he swung her up into his arms, and carried her to his bedroom. The masculine furnishings were so like Dex that she immediately felt safe and warm. He shoved the quilt back and eased her onto his bed.

Hunger darkened his eyes, and he parted his lips, his breath ragged. "I need you, too, Melissa."

She licked her lips and reached for him and he came into her arms. They tore at each other's clothes, hungry for each other's touch, inhibitions floating away as the blissful memory of making love to Dex washed over her.

Dex tossed his jeans to the floor, and looked down at her with the kind of passion that made her body tingle all over. She was naked and aching for him, and she ran her finger over his broad chest, telling him with her eyes how much she wanted him.

A wicked smile curved his mouth, and he crawled above her and angled his head for another kiss. Deep, hungry, it seared her to her soul.

She threaded her fingers into his hair, kissing him back with all the love in her heart. The kiss seemed to last forever but not long enough. It would never be enough.

Need built as he planted kisses down her throat again, then he tugged one bare nipple into his mouth and suckled her. A shiver rippled through her, and he teased the other nipple with his fingers until she clawed at his back.

She wrapped her leg around his, stroking his calf with one foot as he moved above her. His thick length teased her thigh. Heat flared in every cell in her body.

He was relentless in tormenting her and trailed hungry kisses from her breasts to her belly.

She wanted him inside her.

But he shoved her legs apart with a groan, then dove his tongue inside her heat. He licked and sucked at her secret places until the tendrils of an orgasm began to rock through her.

"Dex," she moaned.

He rose above her, yanked on a condom, then thrust inside her. Melissa wrapped her legs around his hips, clawing at his back as he drove himself deep inside her. One thrust, two; he built a rhythm as their bodies joined together.

DEX WANTED TO prolong the pleasure, but making love to Melissa ignited every need in his body. Desire and passion swamped him as she lifted her hips and allowed him to move deeper inside her.

Her whispered moans of pleasure and kisses reminded him of how precious her touch could be. She was lightness to his darkness, a sweet balm to his aching soul.

She raked her hands down his bare back, clinging to him as he pumped inside her, and arousing him to the point of no return. Erotic sensations exploded through his body, and he murmured her name as his release claimed him.

She joined him, riding the waves of pleasure again, and crying out as another orgasm rocked through her.

His heart raced, his body shuddering against hers. He cradled her in his arms and rolled them to his side, holding her close and kissing her hair as the pleasure slowly subsided. A quick trip to the bathroom to dispose of the condom, and he crawled back in bed with her.

His desire hadn't subsided at all, though. Instead it possessed him with an intensity he'd never experienced.

He wanted her again. And again. And again.

Tonight, tomorrow…maybe always…

The thought sent a bolt of fear through him. He'd never felt this way about a woman. Had always loved 'em and walked away.

No…he'd never really loved them. He'd had sex; no love was involved.

Melissa snuggled next to him with her head on his chest, and emotions filled him. Tonight, with her, was not just sex.

The thought of anyone hurting her twisted him inside out.

She whispered his name on a breathy sigh, and he hugged her closer, then kissed her deeply. Melissa looped her arms around his neck and climbed on top of him. Hunger stirred in him as her hair brushed his chest. She tortured him with more kisses, then slid down his body, trailing love licks down his chest to his belly.

His stomach clenched, his sex hardening again.

He reached for her arms to roll her over, but she used one hand to stroke him while she ran her tongue down to the tip of his sex. Raw hunger heated his blood.

He moaned her name, and she closed her lips around the tip of him, then tormented him with her fingers and her tongue until another orgasm built.

He'd forgotten how insatiable Melissa had been. But he didn't intend to leave her behind. He pulled her above him, settling her hips on top of him and gripping them to guide her on his thick erection. Her warm wet center drew him in, and he groaned, hunger begging him to take her hard and fast. She matched passion at every level, the soft mounds of her breasts screaming for him to touch them.

He cupped them in his hands, massaging her weight, then teased her turgid nipples with his fingers and tongue until she moaned with pleasure. She lifted her hips, pulling away from him, then lowered herself again, impaling herself on him. Over and over.

Her body hugged his throbbing sex, milking him as she rode him up and down. Passion built again, and he clutched her hips, then thrust deeper and deeper until she called his name in a rush of blinding pleasure that sent them both over the edge. She clung to him while the sensations ebbed and flowed, their breathing erratic but slowly settling into a steady rhythm that filled him with a kind of peace he hadn't felt in a long time.

When they'd made love years ago, the passion had

been intense, but he'd been too afraid to allow emotions into the mix. Too focused on the pain of his past and what he was going to do with his life.

Melissa had a way of soothing that pain. She made him want to think about a future.

A future that involved more than work and solving cases and running from someone who might care for him.

She made him want to take a chance on love. On them.

His throat clogged with emotions, robbing him of his words. He couldn't make any declarations or promises to her until his life was in order. Until he knew who killed his father and who'd been preying on the homeless men.

It was the only way to keep Melissa safe. And keeping her safe meant more to him than anything.

CONTENT IN DEX'S ARMS, Melissa slept like she hadn't slept in ages. She was safe and cared for, and in a place that felt like home.

Sweet images of living with Dex filled her dreams, images of a beautiful wedding on the lawn of the ranch. She wore a long white antique gown, and Dex looked handsome in his duster jacket and cowboy hat. April stood beside her as maid of honor, and Dex's family watched as he held her hand and declared his vows. A tender kiss, then a party to celebrate with his family, then he swept her into his arms and took her home. They made love long into the night, and every night after that, their love growing stronger each day.

Thanksgiving came, and Dex helped her serve meals at the shelter, then Christmas with presents for everyone in need. Then holiday dinners with the Hawks, and a little dark-haired boy with big eyes who followed Dex around like a doting puppy.

She finally belonged somewhere. Was putting down roots. Had stowed her suitcase in the closet to stay. She added some feminine touches to the house, and decorated their son's room. A map on the wall showed the places she'd moved to, while another map of the ranch hung beside it, a reminder that she was finished running.

She'd hand-painted a Home Sweet Home sign that hung over the sofa and planted flowers in the bed in front of the cabin.

Then she was pregnant again, this time with a little girl. Dex was holding her and rubbing her belly, whispering how much he loved her and their family.

Nothing could ever tear them apart.

A loud knocking jerked her from her sleep. Confused and irritated to have her perfect life interrupted, she closed her eyes and ignored it. It was probably down the street.

But reality intruded. No, she wasn't at her bungalow. She was at Dex's. In his arms.

He rolled over with a groan, irritated, too. He dropped a kiss on her cheek, then slid from bed. "I'd better see who that is."

Morning sunlight streamed through the window, a reminder that her blissful night was over. Gunther was dead. Dex's father had been murdered.

And her dream had been just that—a dream.

DEX STUMBLED FROM BED, still groggy from sleep and hating to leave Melissa. She'd felt so damn good next to him and in his arms that he wanted to stay there forever.

The knocking that woke him grew louder. He yanked on a pair of jeans and a T-shirt and padded barefoot to the front door.

"Dex, it's me, Lamar."

Maybe he had news. He opened the door, anxious to hear what his friend had to say.

"You're here early. It's must be important," Dex said.

Lamar's stern expression confirmed that it was. He stepped into the cabin, his shoulders squared.

"You want coffee?" Dex asked.

Lamar narrowed his eyes at Dex, taking in his state of dress. "Sure. And you're definitely going to want some."

Dex stepped over to the kitchen and started a pot to brew. Behind him, he felt Melissa's presence and glanced sideways to see her standing in the doorway. Her hair looked rumpled, but she'd dressed. "Something wrong?"

A vein bulged in Lamar's forehead. Not a good sign. "I have to talk to you about your father's death, Dex. Maybe we should do it in private."

Dex shook his head. "You can say whatever you have to say in front of Melissa."

A flash of irritation in Lamar's eyes indicated he didn't approve, but he shrugged and laid a folder on the table.

He waited until Dex poured mugs of coffee for everyone and Dex and Melissa gathered at the table.

Dex's stomach clenched. "So what is it?"

"You're right, Dex. Your father was murdered."

Dex steeled himself against a reaction. "What changed your mind?"

"I have proof," Lamar said.

"What kind of proof?"

Lamar opened the folder, then laid a medical report on the table. "The DNA from that bloody rag matched Smith's."

Melissa gasped. "That can't be true."

"Forensics doesn't lie," Lamar said bluntly. "And neither do these." He removed several photographs and spread them across the table. "I had our tech pull pics from security cameras around the city and she found these."

Lamar gestured to a set of pictures showing Smith at the vet's, then near the stall where the man was gored by the bull. Another pic showed Smith standing over Gunther with a gun.

Melissa shook her head in denial and rubbed her hand over her eyes.

Two more photographs showed Smith with Harry Willis. Then there was a picture of Harry's dead body.

"His body was found last night in a wooded section not far from the vet's farm. Just like your friend Gunther, Ms. Gentry, he was shot."

Pain wrenched Melissa's face.

Then Lamar produced another set of photos. Photos of Smith with Dex's father.

In the first one, Smith and his father were in an alley. The next one showed the two of them hunched over a fire built in a garbage can. Then one of Smith by the pickup truck his father had crashed.

Smith was holding a liquor bottle in his hand, exactly like the one that had been on the seat beside his father's dead body.

Chapter Twenty-One

Dex's mind raced as he struggled to assimilate what he was seeing with Smith's story. Had it all been lies? Was his amnesia an act?

"I still don't believe it," Melissa said. "Jim doesn't seem like a cold-blooded killer. He kept to himself, but he made friends with the other men at the shelter."

Dex couldn't contain his fury. Smith had killed his father; that was cold-blooded to him. "Stop defending him, Melissa."

"He made friends with them so he could use them," Lamar said curtly.

"What are you talking about?" Melissa asked.

"I have a theory," Lamar said. "Smith paid the men a small amount of money to buy cattle at auction at a low price. That way the deals couldn't be traced back to him. Then he had Dr. Huckleberry fake papers showing that they were stud quality, and turned around and sold them for major bucks."

"And he killed the homeless men so they couldn't reveal their connection to him or what he was doing," Dex interjected.

"Exactly."

"If he made all this money as you suggest," Melissa said, "then why was he staying at the shelter?"

"To hide out," Lamar said.

"But Jim claims he was injured, that he lost his memory," Melissa argued.

"A story he concocted to cover his tracks," Lamar said.

"You think Baxter was in on it?" Dex asked.

Lamar began stacking the pictures back inside the folder. "There's no proof that he was. I think it was all Smith's scheme."

Dex rubbed his forehead. "So who took these pictures, and why didn't he or she stop the murders?"

"They were sent in anonymously," Lamar said. "My people are trying to track down the source."

"I want to show the photographs to Lucas. Maybe he can help us find out if Baxter was involved or who took them."

Lamar nodded, then addressed Melissa. "Do you know how to contact Smith?"

Melissa folded her arms around her waist. "No. He doesn't have a cell phone."

"That you know of," Lamar said. "He probably uses burner phones so they can't be traced."

Melissa shrugged. "I never saw him use one."

"You saw what he wanted you to see, Miss Gentry." This time Lamar's tone sounded sympathetic. "I'm sorry. But these types of people prey on innocent and trusting souls like you."

Dex clamped his teeth together. Lamar was right.

Melissa glanced at Dex. "You can drop me at the shelter. If he comes there, I'll call you."

"That's not a bad idea," Lamar said. "We could stake out the place and catch him when he shows up."

"No." A mixture of anger and fear hardened Dex's tone. "It's too dangerous."

Sympathy blended with Lamar's brusque, business-like tone. "If you want to catch the man who murdered your father, this is our best chance, Dex."

"Trust me, Dex. He won't hurt me," Melissa said.

"It has nothing to do with trust," Dex said bluntly. "He's a killer, Melissa. There's no way we're using you as a pawn. If he knows we're onto his scheme, then he might turn on you."

DEX'S STEELY LOOK warned Melissa there was no use in arguing with him. She understood his concerns. And the detective had made a good case against Jim Smith.

But her instincts whispered that they were wrong.

Maybe she was a fool. A sucker. But something about Jim had gotten under her skin. The way he'd protected her when McTruitt had put that gun to her said he wouldn't kill innocent, vulnerable men for money.

It hurt that Dex didn't trust her. Although his emotions had to be in a tangle because this investigation was personal. How could she blame him?

He'd learned that the father he'd wanted to reconcile with for nearly twenty years had been murdered. And Lamar presented evidence that Smith had killed him.

"Stay here and get some rest," Dex told her. "Lamar and I are going to see Lucas. Maybe we can figure out a plan to catch Smith." Her earlier offer hung in the air between them. He didn't intend to change his mind.

"I need to go home," Melissa said.

"I'll take you after we finish at Lucas's."

She nodded, and decided to grab a shower while he was gone. Dex and Lamar headed outside, and she went to look out the window. The sun streaked the lush green pastures, and two beautiful black stallions galloped on a hill in the distance. Hawk's Landing was so serene and picturesque that it could have been a postcard advertising for Texas.

She studied Dex's furnishings again. The crocheted afghan over the couch, the stacked-stone fireplace that ran from floor to ceiling, the pictures of his family on the mantel. She walked over and studied each of them. She recognized his brothers from the news in the last year, and picked out Honey and Charlotte and Dr. Mila Manchester.

Dex's mother was surrounded by several teenage girls who, thanks to her loving care, looked bubbly and happy, not traumatized and beaten down from their ordeal with the human trafficking ring.

Each of the men in the family fought to protect and serve in their own way. They wore their badge of justice like an honor. Yet, instead of hardening their attitudes, they valued families and helping others.

She'd always yearned to belong somewhere, to have a family. But as much as she loved Dex, he'd left her before, and he probably would again.

Maybe if she could help find his father's killer, he could finally find some peace in his life. That could be her parting gift before she moved on. And it was time…

She padded to the bathroom, stripped and turned on the shower. The warm spray felt heavenly, yet as the water cascaded down her skin, she closed her eyes and could still feel Dex's fingers on her body, teasing and tormenting her and bringing her pleasure. She'd never forgotten his touch.

She never would.

When the water grew cool, she slipped from the shower and dried off, wishing she had another change of clothes, but these would have to do. Her cell phone was ringing as she finished dressing.

Expecting April or Dex to be calling, she rushed to answer it.

"Hello."

"Melissa, this is Jim."

Her heart stuttered. "Hey. Listen, that detective was here. He has pictures of you and Dex's father and he's saying that you killed him."

"I didn't," Jim said. "But pieces of my past have been coming back. I think they may be important."

"Tell me more."

"Some are about the place where I was knocked out, where I lost my memory."

"What do you remember about it?"

"Everything's still foggy," he said. "I'd like to go back to the place. I think it might jog my memory."

"Do you know where this place is?"

His breath rattled out. "Actually, it's near Hawk's ranch, on the border of it and the Native American reservation."

Melissa inhaled sharply. If he went to the place and remembered who'd assaulted him, maybe he could tell them who was behind the missing homeless men.

"I'm on the ranch now," Melissa said. "I'll go with you."

"That could be dangerous, Melissa."

"I don't care, I believe you're innocent and I want

the truth. Dex deserves it, too. Although coming here will be dangerous for you. That cop is looking for you."

"I have to do this," Jim said. "For myself. I…have to prove I'm not who that detective says I am."

"Then come by and get me."

A tense heartbeat passed. "Are you sure?"

"Yes."

"I'll be there in five minutes."

"I'll be waiting outside." She hung up, grabbed her purse and rushed outside to watch for him. Hopefully he'd arrive before Dex returned. If not, she'd have to think of some way to convince Dex to listen to what Jim had to say.

DEX AND LAMAR met Lucas in his study where Lamar laid out the evidence for Lucas to see.

Lamar explained about the DNA on the bloody rag and relayed his theory as Lucas studied the pictures.

"DNA is damning," Lucas said. "And these photographs certainly do look incriminating."

"I talked to Baxter," Dex said. "He denies any wrongdoing, but seemed nervous when I questioned him."

"He should be nervous," Lucas said. "If we prove cattle were misrepresented at his auction house, word will spread and his reputation will be ruined. He'll probably face lawsuits, and possibly charges."

"Let's not get ahead of ourselves," Lamar said. "At this point, we just need to find Smith and force him to confess."

"You already have every law enforcement agency in Texas looking for Smith," Lucas said.

Lamar explained about wanting to use Melissa to draw Smith out, but Dex vetoed the idea again.

Lucas walked over to the whiteboard he kept in his study, flipped it over and gestured to the information he and Dex had collected regarding the case. Lucas had filled in the blanks with the names and dates of all the missing men he'd discovered in police reports over the past twenty years along with the histories of a few of the men and their families.

The dates that two of the men disappeared were only months before his father abandoned them. Could his disappearance have been connected to the missing men?

If he'd learned something about them, why hadn't he gone to the sheriff?

And why hadn't Smith killed him eighteen years ago instead of waiting until now?

"Did Smith indicate where he might go?" Lamar asked.

Dex shook his head.

"What exactly did he tell you?" Lucas asked. "Other than the story about having amnesia? How and where did he lose his memory?"

Dex replayed their conversation in his head. "On some land, near a rock formation. He said that when he regained consciousness, there were arrowheads everywhere."

Lucas drummed his fingers on his desk. "Dex, that sounds like that formation on the edge of our property. The one that borders the land owned by the rez."

Dex nodded. "You're right. I remember us hiking out there with Dad when we were little. He brought us some arrowheads he found there. That's what sparked my interest, and then Chrissy and I started collecting them."

"If Smith lost his memory there, he might return," Lucas suggested.

"Or if he's been hiring guns to cover up his scheme," Lamar cut in, "maybe that's their meeting spot."

Dex's heart pounded. "You're right. I'll check on Melissa, then we'll drive up there."

Lucas pinched the bridge of his nose. "Charlotte had some more Braxton-Hicks contractions last night, so I don't want to leave her alone. Let me take her to the house to stay with Mom, then I'll meet you at your cabin and we'll ride together."

"Sounds like a plan," Dex agreed.

Lamar's phone buzzed with a text, and he stepped outside on the porch and responded to it. When he finished, Dex hurried to Lamar's vehicle. Lamar started the engine and sped toward Dex's cabin.

Dust drifted in the air near his drive as they rounded the curve. Dex spotted an old black pickup heading away from the cabin in the opposite direction.

Lamar noticed it at the same time. "Is that one of your hands?"

"I don't think so," Dex said. "Stop at the cabin."

Lamar sped down the drive and swung the police car to a halt. Dex jumped out, sprinted up the steps and through the front door. "Melissa, are you here?"

His pulse clamored as he raced through the house. Melissa's coffee mug sat on the kitchen table, but her purse was gone. He checked the bedroom, then the kitchen again and found a note on the counter near the coffeepot.

Dear Dex,
I know you don't trust Jim, but I do. I'm going
with him to the rocks to see if it will jog his mem-
ory. He wants to know the truth the same as you
and I do.

Love, Melissa

Dex punched Melissa's number, and it rang several times, but she didn't answer. Dammit.

He raced back outside. Lamar was waiting by the car, a cigarette in his hand. Odd, he thought his friend had quit.

"She's gone," he said as he jumped back in the passenger side. "Let's go."

Lamar stubbed the cigarette on the ground and climbed in, a scowl deepening the frown lines on his face. "Where?"

Dex gestured toward the road. "To the rocks. Smith was in that truck and Melissa's with him."

MELISSA RODE IN silence as Jim drove from Hawk's Landing onto the bordering property, just over the line onto the reservation. The area was miles and miles from the houses and buildings that the natives inhabited, deserted, and out of sight from the highway.

A frisson of nerves rippled through her. If Jim was lying and wanted to hurt her, this would be a perfect place to do so. No one would find her.

But one look at his troubled expression, and a calmness overcame her. So far, her instincts hadn't failed her at the shelters. She wouldn't ignore them now. He didn't plan to hurt her. He wanted her help.

Jim parked beneath a cluster of trees, between a cactus and a boulder that shielded the truck from the road. He turned to her, his dark gaze serious. "I was here."

He gestured toward the rock formation. "Over there." They sat for a long moment in silence while he seemed to be reliving a memory of the past.

His breathing grew unsteady, and he opened the truck door and got out. Melissa watched. She had to be patient and not pressure him to remember.

Quietly, she slid from the truck and followed him.

Just as he'd said, the rocks were shaped like an arrow. Gravel crunched beneath her shoes, and she looked down and saw dozens of arrowheads on the ground. Dex had a collection on his wall.

Suddenly Jim made a low sound in his throat, then placed one hand on the top of the rocks. His face turned ashen.

She inched forward to see what he was looking at and froze. Dear God. There were mounds of dirt lined up on the other side of the rocks.

Mounds that looked like graves.

Chapter Twenty-Two

Dex texted Lucas and asked him to meet them at the rocks. Fear for Melissa warred with anger. Why hadn't she called him to tell him about Smith?

Unless the man had taken her against her will…

But her note indicated that she'd gone of her own volition.

Hell, Smith could have held a gun on her and forced her to write the note.

Lamar kept a pair of binoculars in his dash, so Dex grabbed them and used them to track the pickup truck as they crested the hill. Smith had parked between a boulder and cactus, hidden. Of course, he was in hiding. He knew good and damn well the cops were after him.

And he had Melissa with him.

Lamar slowed and approached to the left, then parked off the side of the road at the bottom of the hill but far enough away that Smith couldn't see them. The detective pulled his gun as he eased from the unmarked squad car.

Dex joined him, but held up a finger signaling they had to talk. "Lamar, we have to approach with caution.

If Smith is armed, we could spook him and he might hurt Melissa."

Lamar glared at him. "Listen, Dex. I'm in charge here. You are to let me take the lead."

"Right." But Lamar didn't care about Melissa personally the way he did. "Please, I just don't want her to be hurt."

Lamar's gaze met his, understanding in his eyes. "I know you're in love with her. I'll do all I can to keep her safe." He gestured toward the rocks. "Now, let's go get your father's killer."

Adrenaline spiked as they crept through the bushes toward the rocks. When they reached a small hill that offered a view of Smith and Melissa, he used his binoculars to see if Smith was armed.

"No weapon," Dex muttered.

"Don't get comfortable. He could have it hidden," Lamar said.

Dex peered through the binoculars again and focused on Melissa's face. She looked pale, nervous, as if she was afraid.

Had Smith threatened her? Was he using her as a hostage?

Smith walked a few feet around the rocks, then stooped down beside a mound of dirt. He ran his fingers over the mound, stirring dust, then picked up an arrowhead and studied it.

Melissa remained frozen, shock streaking her face.

Dex inched forward, straining to get a better look. There was another mound beside the first. Then another.

"Dammit," Dex muttered. "Those mounds—"

"Are graves," Lamar said. "We have him now. Smith led us straight to the bodies of some of his victims."

MELISSA COUNTED FIVE mounds of dirt. Five graves. Had Jim known they were here?

He reached into his pocket, and her breath caught. Did he have a gun? Could she be wrong about him?

She started to back away. Her phone was in her purse in the truck. She could call Dex.

But Jim didn't make a move toward her. His hand slid from his pocket. Instead of a gun, he held a small object, maybe a coin? He rubbed it between his fingers as he stared at the graves. His eyes looked vacant, lost in thought, his posture rigid and tense.

A slight breeze stirred the hot air. She inhaled dust as it swirled around her feet. Jim stooped down and raked at the dirt near one of the graves. What was he doing?

"I was here," he said in a low voice. "This is where it happened. Where I lost my past."

Melissa clenched her hands together. "What else do you remember?"

He angled his head toward the sun, squinting, then at the rocks as if struggling for details. Then he looked at the object in his hand and studied it.

"I came out here to meet someone," he said. "About a deal. Then I found these graves. And then…something hard slammed into the back of my head."

She sucked in a breath. "Someone knocked you out because you found the graves. Did you see who it was?"

He shook his head, his expression tormented. "But I knew something was wrong before he hit me. Before I found the graves. That's the reason I came out here."

A noise, rocks skittering behind her, jerked Melissa's attention to the space to the right of Jim. Dex was perched behind a boulder holding a gun.

"You knew where those bodies were buried because you put them there," Dex growled.

Smith swung his gaze toward Dex, his fingers stroking that coin. But it wasn't a real coin, it was wooden.

"No," Jim said. "I don't think that's what happened. I… I figured out that something was wrong—"

"What are you talking about?" Dex asked.

Jim lifted the wooden coin. Dex's eyes widened. "A wooden nickel. My daddy always told me…"

"Not to take any wooden nickels," Dex finished at the same time Jim muttered the phrase.

Jim nodded. "But I did. I realized I had."

Melissa's head swam as she tried to follow the conversation.

"What do you mean?" she asked softly. "Someone gave you that wooden nickel?"

He shook his head again. "No, the saying, it means don't let anyone cheat you. But I did." He paused, then his eyes lit up as if remembering something. "I bought a bull, thought it was a prize one, but when I went to register it, I learned it wasn't. I'd been conned."

"Someone conned you or you were the one doing the con?" Dex asked.

"I was conned. I went to the auction house to confront the auctioneer and overheard some men talking." He paused, then pinched the bridge of his nose in thought. "They were talking about how they did it."

"You mean how you did it." The detective suddenly appeared beside Melissa, his weapon aimed at Jim. "You came up with the idea. You paid homeless men to buy them cheap at auction, then forged papers to make the bulls look like stud quality and resold at a higher price." Detective Lamar heaved a breath. "Then you killed the men who helped you and buried them here just like you killed Steven Hawk and Gunther and Harry Willis and Dr. Huckleberry to cover your tracks."

The detective stepped forward, clenching his gun tighter. "Now, put your hands up. You're under arrest."

Jim raised his hands, but a challenging look glinted in his eyes. "You can take me in, but I remember what happened now. I didn't kill these men, but I know who did."

"You can give your statement when we get to the station," Detective Lamar snapped.

Dex moved from behind the rock where he'd been standing. "I want to hear what he says right now." Dex aimed his weapon at Smith. "Did you kill my father?"

"No," Smith said. "I didn't kill anyone. I told you I was attacked."

"Tell us what happened," Melissa said softly.

Dex held his breath while he waited on Smith to explain. The man kept rubbing that wooden nickel, stirring childhood memories for Dex.

Smith claimed he'd been attacked in this spot, on the border of Hawk's Landing and the rez. Had his father stumbled onto what Smith was doing eighteen years ago?

Dex slid one hand into his pocket, his fingers running over the wooden nickel his father had given him. The wooden nickel...the saying...it was exactly what his father used to tell him.

Questions clanged around in his head. Questions that made no sense and seemed too coincidental to believe.

But they planted themselves in his mind anyway. Had Smith stolen the wooden nickel from his father?

Dex narrowed his eyes. "When exactly did you lose your memory?"

Smith looked down at the wooden nickel, then back at Dex, then at Lamar. "Ask your friend. He was here."

Stunned, Dex narrowed his eyes. "What the hell are you talking about?"

"Ask him," Smith said sharply.

Dex glanced at Lamar. Something akin to panic streaked his face, then Lamar suddenly bolted to the side, grabbed Melissa and shoved his gun to her head. "I'm sorry, Dex. It wasn't supposed to happen like this."

Melissa shrieked, and Dex's pulse jumped with fear. For a brief second, he couldn't move. Couldn't speak.

Smith claimed Lamar was dirty. But Lamar had been his friend…his mentor…he'd stood by him at his father's funeral…

God…all these years he'd stayed in touch with the family. Had promised that he'd never stop looking for their father.

"Lamar, tell me it's not true." Emotions thickened Dex's throat as a possible scenario formed in his mind.

"I'm sorry, Dex," Lamar said, his brows furrowing. "I really am. I never meant for it to happen, but I was young and desperate for money. At first, it just seemed like an easy way to make some cash. All I had to do was to turn a blind eye to what Baxter was doing."

"So Baxter was behind the scam?" Dex said.

"He was trying to save his ranch," Lamar said.

"And the man who broke into my house," Melissa said. "Was he working for Baxter?"

Lamar nodded. "Yeah, he was supposed to take care of you."

"Why did you kill him?" Dex asked. "To cover up for Baxter?"

"Damn fool was about to leave without finishing the job."

"So you've been working for Baxter all this time," Dex said.

Lamar shrugged. "When I first realized what he was up to, I was going to arrest him, but then he offered me a lot of money to keep quiet. It was just cattle. The men who were buying it could afford it. No one was supposed to get hurt."

"But he used homeless men and then killed them," Smith cut in.

Lamar glared at Smith. "By the time I figured that out, I was in too deep. He threatened to take me down with him. I couldn't let that happen. I was in my twenties, I couldn't spend my life in prison."

"So how did my father play into it?" Dex asked. "Did you try to kill him, too? Or did you threaten to hurt us if he talked? Is that why he left? To protect my family from you?"

MELISSA TRIED TO loosen the detective's grip around her neck, but he wrapped his arm tighter around her throat, and she felt the cold barrel of the gun dig into her temple. One slip of his finger and she'd be dead.

Betrayal darkened Dex's eyes. Jim stood stock-still, his posture braced to fight. But he was holding back just as Dex was.

"Please don't do this," she whispered to the detective. "Dex is your friend."

"I'm sorry," Detective Lamar murmured. "But I can't go to prison."

Lucas Hawk appeared from behind a boulder and inched up beside Dex, his weapon drawn. "That's exactly where you're going."

"No, I'm not," the detective barked.

"I knew the minute I saw those photographs that they were fake," Lucas said. "You had them photoshopped to frame this man." He pointed toward Jim. "Because you're the one who knocked him out years ago. You're the reason he lost his memory."

At least Lucas believed Jim.

A muscle ticked in Lucas's jaw. "Drop the gun, Lamar, and let Melissa go."

Lamar shook his head and dragged her backward toward the rocks. "Come any closer and I'll kill her right here."

Melissa's gaze met Dex's. She didn't want to die.

Chapter Twenty-Three

Rage at Lamar coiled inside Dex. This man had pretended to be his friend, but he'd lied to him to cover up his criminal activities. He'd conspired to murder numerous men and was framing Smith for it. Just how far did his deception go?

"You killed Gunther, didn't you?" Melissa cried. "Why? He was trying to get his life together."

"He was coming to tell you what was going on," Lamar said. "I warned him not to, but he wouldn't listen. Damn old man had a conscience."

Dex cleared his throat. "And the man in the truck, my father, you killed him for the same reason?"

Lamar nodded. "You should have stopped asking questions then," Lamar said. "I thought you'd finally have closure."

"All I wanted was the truth. But you lied to me and pretended to be my friend."

Lamar tightened his hold on Melissa. "Like I said, you should have let it go, Dex."

Dex hardened himself to the man who'd mentored him. He had Melissa's life in his hands now. Dex would do anything to save her.

"You aren't going to murder her in front of me and an FBI agent," Dex said. "Then you'd have to kill us all."

Indecision flashed on Lamar's face, then panic, and Dex realized that Lamar would do whatever necessary to save himself. What were a few more lives added to the death toll he'd already racked up?

"You won't get away with this," Lucas said. "I've already called for backup and spoken with my superior. You're going down, Lamar. The best thing you can do is to cut a deal with us."

"A deal?" Lamar scoffed. "You mean prison time."

Lucas shrugged. "If you testify against Baxter and give us the names of everyone involved in this operation, you might escape the death penalty."

"Baxter's men would find me, even in jail," Lamar said.

Lucas glanced over his shoulder. "At least release Melissa. Backup will be here any minute. No need in taking any more lives."

Lamar shielded himself with Melissa's body and took another step backward. "You aren't the only one who has backup. If you want your family—and I mean all of your family—to be safe, then arrange for a helicopter for me to leave the country."

Dex's blood ran cold. "What do you mean—all of our family?" Dex asked.

"Baxter has men at your ranch house right now," Lamar said. "No one is safe until I fly out of here."

"You've taken them hostage?" Dex asked, incredulous. Who *was* this man?

Not his friend. He was a liar and a cheat and a murderer.

"This is what you did before," Smith said. "You threatened to hurt them if I talked."

Lamar whirled on him, the gun still pressed against Melissa's temple. "You were never supposed to remember."

"But I do," Smith said. "I remember everything now."

Dex and Lucas exchanged a look. Turmoil darkened Smith's eyes as he looked at the two of them.

"I remember who I am," he said. "I was searching for Chrissy when I stumbled on these bodies. Then I put it all together about the raw deal on the bull."

The blood roared in Dex's ears. "What do you mean? You were looking for Chrissy?" The wooden nickel, the rocks, the arrowheads…

His head spun…could it be true? Could this man be—

"You're our father," Lucas said, voicing the thoughts running through Dex's mind. He shot Lamar an accusatory look. "You faked the DNA report on the man in the pickup to make us think it was our dad," Lucas said to Lamar. "How did you manage that? Did you pay off the ME to fake the autopsy, to say the DNA matched?"

"I didn't have to. I managed to get my hands on Sheriff Dunar's initial files and planted false DNA in there for Dr. Hudson to use for comparison. He really believed the man in the truck was your father."

"That man was just another missing homeless man." Lucas paused. "Good thing, I had my people run Smith's DNA." He pulled his phone from his pocket and held it up. "I just got the results a few minutes ago. It was a match to Steven Hawk's."

Dex's heart was pounding so hard he could barely breathe.

Smith was...his father?

And Lamar had tried to kill him years ago.

And again in the past few weeks just as Smith—his father—had said.

Rage and a sense of betrayal seized Dex.

He hadn't recognized his father because it had been nearly two decades since he'd seen him. And with the silver hair and the scar and missing finger and limp...

Lamar had painted Smith as the dangerous one. And Dex had trusted and believed Lamar...

Instead of caring for his family, Lamar had cozied up to them. He'd pretended to continue the search for Dex's father, but he'd only wanted to make sure he was never found. Or that he never remembered the truth.

"You hired McTruitt to kill me?" Smith—his father—said.

"Damn you. You were getting too close to the truth," Lamar shouted.

"It's over, Lamar," Dex said. "The killing has to stop. You've hurt our family enough."

Lamar was shaking his head, but he looked defeated. Dex crept toward him, determined to get Melissa away from him.

"Don't come any closer," Lamar growled.

Dex stooped slowly and laid his gun on the ground. "I'm not armed." He stood upright, holding his hands in the air in surrender, then took another step. "Let her go and take me as your hostage. Lucas can make the arrangements for the chopper, and I'll fly out with you to make sure you escape." He angled his head to-

ward Lucas. "My brothers won't shoot at you as long
as I'm with you."

"He's right," Lucas says. "You should take him. It's
your only way out, Lamar."

Melissa shook her head at him, mouthing no. He
ignored her. No question in his mind—he'd trade his
life for hers any day.

"Let her go." Dex inched closer, and Lamar shoved
Melissa forward, then aimed the gun at Dex.

His father grabbed Melissa and pulled her behind
the rocks. Lucas remained still, his hand on his phone.
"Stay calm, Lamar. I'm calling to arrange for the chopper."

"Then you have to call the goons off our family,"
Dex snarled.

"When I see the chopper and we're inside," Lamar
snapped. "Not before."

Lucas spoke low into his cell. His expression remained stoic as he lowered the phone. "Done. It'll be
here in a few minutes."

Lamar wiped sweat from his brow, his breathing
shaky as he kept the gun on Dex. Dex was not about
to let him get in a chopper or allow his family to be
killed by Baxter's men.

Smith was still holding Melissa behind the rocks, so
Dex signaled Lucas that he planned to make a move. A
muscle tightened in Lucas's jaw, and he gave a slight
nod.

Dex didn't hesitate. He quickly jabbed his elbow into
Lamar's side and stomped on his instep. Lamar bel-
lowed and jerked to the side, then Lucas fired.

Dex twisted around and saw Lamar clutch his shoulder where he'd been hit. But Lamar was quick to re-

cover and was lowering his gun hand again. No time to waste. Dex threw himself at Lamar, and knocked the gun from his hand.

"Go save the family!" he shouted to Lucas. "Help him, Dad! And get Melissa out of here!"

"On it!" Lucas yelled. "Harrison and Brayden are on the way."

Dex and Lamar rolled on the ground, trading blow for blow. Lucas tossed his handcuffs toward Dex. They hit the ground a few feet from them. Gravel crunched.

Lucas, his father and Melissa scrambled down the hill toward Lucas's vehicle.

Lamar shoved his knee into Dex's chest and rolled him over, but Dex snatched a rock from the ground, bucked Lamar off him and threw him to his back. Then he climbed above him and raised the rock, ready to smash Lamar in the face.

Lamar heaved for a breath, fear in his eyes as he stared up at Dex. "Go ahead," Lamar growled. "I'd rather die than be locked up."

Dex wanted to kill him for what he'd done. Lamar had deprived his family of their father for nearly two decades. Had tried to kill him and stolen his life. He'd lied to Dex and pretended to be a family friend.

All so he could keep his dirty secret safe.

All for money.

Pure hatred and contempt railed inside Dex. His hand shook. He wanted Lamar to pay for what he'd done.

Lamar shot him a challenging look, then grabbed Dex by the throat, trying to choke him.

Dex dropped the rock, jerked the man's hands off

his throat, then punched him in the face so hard blood spurted from Lamar's nose. He'd broken it. Good.

Lamar sputtered, blood gushing. Dex capitalized on the moment, snagged the handcuffs, shoved Lamar to his stomach and handcuffed him. Lamar was cursing and fighting, but a kick to his kidneys quieted the fight from him. Lamar groaned in pain and curled on his side, then passed out.

Dex yanked a zip tie from his pocket and secured Lamar's feet. Then he dragged him toward Lamar's police car. He opened the trunk, hauled Lamar into it and slammed it shut.

Heart racing, he jumped in the driver's seat, started the engine and sped back toward the farmhouse and his family.

Lamar had stolen years of their family's life together. He refused to let him take another minute.

Chapter Twenty-Four

Melissa closed her eyes in prayer as Lucas drove toward the Hawks' main house. *Dear God, please let Dex be okay.*

She opened her eyes and glanced over her shoulder, hoping to see Dex, following them. But nothing...

"Are you okay?" Dex's father asked.

She nodded, although she wouldn't be okay until she knew Dex was safe.

"You remembered everything?" Melissa asked.

He nodded. "I'm Steven Hawk. My family...I lost them..." His voice cracked. "They think I abandoned them?"

Jim Smith was Steven Hawk. That had been a shock.

Compassion for Dex and his family filled her. Detective Lamar had deceived Dex. He had to feel betrayed.

She squeezed Steven's hand. "They love you and never stopped looking for you. They'll understand."

Lucas slowed to a stop by the stable, out of clear sight of the house. His brothers Harrison and Brayden were waiting, both looking worried.

"Stay in the car, Melissa." Lucas turned to his father. "You, too, Dad."

Steven shook his head. "No way. I lost my family once. I'm not going to let anyone hurt them now."

Tears blurred her eyes at the determination and love in his voice. She searched for Dex again as Steven and Lucas climbed from the car.

A gunman stepped from inside the farmhouse onto the porch. He was standing guard, on the lookout for trouble.

Was there another man with the family? Were the foster girls inside?

Lucas and his brothers and father hovered together by the stable. They shared an emotional moment as Harrison and Brayden realized their father was standing in front of them. Brief hugs went around.

But there wasn't time for a big reconciliation yet. The family in the house were in danger.

Finally a car sounded in the distance, and she glanced back and saw the detective's car flying down the road.

Nerves ricocheted through her. Was Dex or the detective driving?

DEX FLEW DOWN the road to the farmhouse, his pulse hammering. At least Melissa was safe. But his mother, the foster girls, Charlotte and whoever else was inside... maybe Honey and the baby, and Mila and her little girl, Izzy...everyone the family loved and cared about was in that house.

Dex spotted his brothers and his father by the stable, then searched for Melissa. Thank goodness she was in Lucas's SUV.

He parked behind the stable, then eased around to the side where his brothers had met. Harrison and

Brayden looked shell-shocked as they studied their father, but Lucas was laying out a plan of action.

"Backup is on the way," Lucas said. "Where's Lamar?"

"Unconscious but secure in the trunk of his car." Dex used the binoculars to gain a better view of the house. "I see one guy on the porch. There must be others inside."

Harrison raised a brow, but pulled his gun and checked it for ammo. "The question is how many?"

"We'll find out." Lucas handed each of them a small microphone to attach to their shirt collars and they quickly prepared for a team approach.

"Hold fire until we see what we're dealing with," Lucas said.

Dex and his brothers and father nodded agreement, then Lucas gestured it was time to move. They dispersed, hunching down and running toward opposite sides of the house to assess the situation.

Harrison eased around to the back, while he and Brayden moved to the sides of the house to look inside. Lucas and their father situated themselves behind a tree to watch the gunman on the front porch.

Dex peered into the living room. One gunman with a rifle standing guard over the family. His mother, the foster girls, Honey and the baby, Charlotte, Mila and Izzy were all crouched together on the sofa and chairs. The foster girls looked frightened, and had sidled close to his mother. Honey was patting little Steven on her shoulder, while Charlotte's face looked strained as if she was in pain. Mila sat beside Charlotte, stroking her back and talking in a low voice.

Dear Lord, was Charlotte in labor?

"Kitchen is clear," Harrison said over the mic.

"So are the bedrooms," Brayden said.

Dex swallowed the fear gnawing at him. He had to be calm. Save his family. "They're in the den. One gunman with a rifle. Mom, the girls, Honey and the baby, Charlotte, Mila and Izzy—they're all there."

Lucas cursed. "Anyone hurt?"

Dex didn't know whether to tell him his suspicions about Charlotte or not. "No. Scared, but everyone appears unharmed."

His brothers murmured sounds of relief.

"I'm going after the one on the porch," Lucas said in a low voice. "Just keep watch and make sure there isn't another shooter outside or in another room."

"Copy that," Dex and his brothers murmured.

Dex kept his eyes glued on the family as the gunman paced back and forth in front of the women and children. Bastard. He deserved to die for frightening them.

Seconds later, grunts echoed from the front of the house. The gunman inside paused and jerked his head toward the sound, his gun raised. Dex wanted to burst through the window and tackle him, but that would be too dangerous. If the gun went off, someone could get hurt.

"One down," Lucas said a minute later. "Unconscious, tied up by the porch. Now for the inside man."

A shout echoed from the front. His father.

What the hell was he doing?"

"Dammit, Dad knocked on the door," Lucas said.

He was going to distract the second gunman, draw him out. But what if he got shot and died this time?

"Gunman heading toward the door now," Dex said. "Dammit, he has Mom with him."

The next few minutes raced by in a blur of action. "He's at the door with Dad," Lucas said. "Everyone move in."

Harrison and Brayden shouted they were storming the back, and Dex rushed in the side door through the hall to the den.

"He has Ava," Honey cried.

"I know, Lucas is at the door with them now."

Charlotte cried out in pain, and Mila stroked her hair away from her face. "She's about to have this baby."

Harrison burst in and raced to Honey and the baby while Brayden rushed to Mila. "Are you okay?"

"Yes, but I have a baby to deliver." Mila gestured to the girls. "Get some blankets and clean towels. Hurry!"

A gunshot sounded from the front. Everyone froze. "Stay here," Dex ordered.

Dex eased through the house to the front. The screened door stood open, a body on the floor of the porch. Lucas stood over it while his father stood by Lucas. "He's dead," Lucas said.

His mother was crouched against the wall inside by the door, shaking.

Dex put his arms around her. "It's okay, Mom, it's over. Everyone's safe."

She leaned against him, wiped her eyes and straightened. "Lucas, Charlotte's in labor," she shouted.

Panic flashed in Lucas's eyes, and he raced past Dex to go to Charlotte.

His father had stepped into the entryway, emotions straining his face as he looked past Dex at his mother.

"Ava?" his father murmured.

His mother's eyes flared with emotions. "Steven?"

He nodded, a tear slipping down his cheek.

His mother didn't hesitate. She dove into Dex's father's arms, and they kissed and hugged and cried.

Emotions overcame Dex. His father was home. His family was back together and safe.

Except the woman he loved was in the car waiting, alone.

RELIEF FILLED MELISSA as Dex walked down the porch toward her. Another car screeched up in the drive, and a female and male in suits climbed out.

Dex strode toward them, and Melissa slid from the vehicle. The male identified himself and the female as FBI agents.

"Agent Hawk called for backup," the female agent said.

Dex nodded, and Harrison hurried down the steps and crossed to them.

"We secured the scene and took two gunmen out," Dex said.

"Agent Hawk is a little busy right now," Harrison told the agents. "His wife is giving birth."

Melissa gaped at Dex. Charlotte was having her baby now?

"An ambulance is on the way." Harrison gestured toward the dead man on the porch and the unconscious man tied up on the ground. "So is the ME."

Dex pointed toward the detective's car. "Detective Lamar is inside the trunk, secure. He has a gunshot wound to the shoulder so will need medical aid."

Harrison explained about Lamar's involvement with the scam involving Baxter.

"Lucas filled us in when he called. We have agents

at Baxter's ranch now," the male agent said. "We'll take care of Detective Lamar and the two gunmen."

Brayden rushed onto the front porch. "The baby's here!"

"Come on, Melissa." Dex tugged at her hand. "I want you to meet the family."

Melissa resisted a step. "It's family time, Dex. I'll just get a ride home."

"You're not leaving right now. Everyone is going to want to thank you for bringing Dad back to us." He pulled her hand, and she followed, nerves bunching in her belly as they stepped inside.

"Everyone's in the den with Charlotte and the baby," Brayden said.

Tears stung Melissa's eyes at the tender way Steven and Dex's mother were holding on to each other.

Steven was cradling a baby in a blue blanket, obviously Harrison and Honey's baby boy whom they'd named after him. Lucas hovered on the couch by Charlotte, a beaming smile on his face.

"It's a girl," Lucas said.

Charlotte looked up, blankets covering her as she held the newborn to her chest. "We're going to name her Christine and call her Chrissy."

The Hawks cheered, and the young teens sang out the baby's name from the corner of the room where one of them bounced a little girl about three on her hip. That must be Izzy, Mila's daughter.

When the cheers settled down, Dex cleared his throat and introduced her. "This is Melissa Gentry. Without her, we wouldn't have Dad back."

"I didn't do anything," Melissa said. "He was looking for you all along, weren't you, Jim—I mean, Steven?"

Steven wrapped one arm around his wife and rocked his grandson in his arms. "You believed in me, Melissa. All those years I couldn't remember what had happened or who I was. I started to wonder if I was a bad guy. But you made me believe that I wasn't."

Melissa blinked back tears. For some reason, Jim— Steven—had felt like a father to her. Maybe that was why she couldn't believe anything bad about him.

The next few minutes were chaotic as the family hugged and congratulated Charlotte and Lucas. They also hugged and thanked her.

Still, she felt like an outsider with this close-knit family. They needed and deserved time alone to celebrate Steven's homecoming.

She told Dex that she needed to go the shelter and meet April so they could reopen.

"I'll drive you," Dex offered.

She shook her head. "No, you need to be with your family. You all have a lot of time to make up for."

Emotions brimmed in Dex's eyes. "I don't know how to thank you, Melissa. You saved our family and brought Dad back to us."

She blinked back tears. She didn't want his thanks. She wanted his love.

But she bit her tongue to keep from admitting that, and asked to borrow his car instead. Dex handed her the keys, and their fingers brushed.

A tingle rippled through her, and she tried to memorize his touch. It would probably be the last time she'd feel it.

Tears blurred her eyes as she climbed in his vehicle and started out for home. Her heart was breaking. This was the very reason she didn't get involved.

The reason she'd moved so much. The reason she shouldn't have fallen in love with Dex again.

He belonged here with the Hawks. They had eighteen years to make up for.

She wasn't part of this family and never would be.

Time for her to pack that suitcase and move on.

Chapter Twenty-Five

Dex didn't want Melissa to leave, but the ambulance arrived for Charlotte and the baby, and Harrison was dealing with the agents. Inside, his family was still reeling from the fact that Steven Hawk was alive.

And home.

Lucas and Steven hugged in an emotional moment as the medics loaded Charlotte and baby Chrissy to transport to the hospital. Mila assured them everything was fine with mother and daughter, but still wanted routine tests run on the baby.

"Dad, you should get checked out, too," Dex said.

"I'm fine." Steven waved off his concern. "My memories are back. And I'm home."

"I hate to leave right now," Lucas said to Steven. "We've missed you, Dad. And I want to hear everything that happened to you."

"We have time," their father said. "I'm proud of you and your brothers, son. Thank you for taking care of your mother all these years." Their father wiped at his eyes. "Now, go with your wife and my granddaughter. This time, I'll be here when you return." He glanced toward the house. "As long as your mama still wants me."

"She does," Dex assured him.

Lucas hugged Steven again and hurried to join Charlotte and the baby while the medic examined Lamar. The agents kept him handcuffed and would escort him to the hospital to have the bullet removed, then a trial and prison were waiting.

Bitterness tasted ugly in Dex's mouth. Just what Lamar deserved.

When the agents and ambulances left, he and Harrison joined the family inside. His mother opened her arms and welcomed their father home as if their love had never died.

Dex wanted that kind of love. He thought he had it with Melissa.

Only she'd seemed anxious to leave.

Emotions warred inside him, but their mother wanted answers, so he and his father explained the events that had torn their father from the family all these years.

Then he and his brothers and mother spent the next few hours filling their father in on everything that had happened on the ranch, how the foster girls had come to live with them, how Harrison, Lucas and Brayden had met their wives. How they'd begun to develop the ranch into a working business again.

"We've only just begun," Brayden said.

Their father looked down at their mother, another tear slipping down his scarred face "I missed so much, so many years with you. And the boys growing up. I...don't want to miss any more time with you guys."

"Hawk's Landing is your ranch," Dex said. "Dad, we need you around here."

Their mother pressed a kiss to her husband's cheek.

"Yes, we do, Steven. I've been lost without you. Tell me you're home for good."

"I am if you'll have me, if you'll forgive me..." his voice broke, emotions overtaking him.

Ava drew him into an embrace. "There's nothing to forgive." She placed her hand over her heart. "I never thought you abandoned us. Your place is right here."

More laughter and chatter followed, and drinks were poured to toast. But as they toasted the family, Dex felt an ache deep in his soul.

Someone was missing. Melissa. She belonged here with him.

His father cornered him by the bar. "I owe Melissa so much, Dex. If it wasn't for her generous heart, I might have never remembered and come home."

"I know," Dex said. "She stole a part of my heart, too."

"Then where is she?" his father asked. "Because take a lesson from your old man. Time is precious. Love can be taken away in a heartbeat." He glanced lovingly at his wife. "Some of us get second chances, though. If you love Melissa, go after her, son. Don't waste a minute."

Dex hugged his father, then pounded him on the back. "You're right. She belongs here with me." He gestured around the room. "With all of us. But I hate to leave you when you just got here, Dad." Guilt nagged at him. "I'm sorry for not trusting you. For believing Lamar over you."

Forgiveness blended with love in his father's eyes. "Don't waste time on regrets, either. You thought I was dead. And you had every reason to believe him. You were just a kid when Chrissy disappeared, and when I did, too. You don't deserve to feel guilty."

But he had. And that guilt had hindered him from allowing anyone to get close.

Only Melissa had wormed her way into his heart anyway.

His father was right. He couldn't waste any time on the past. Judging from the way his parents kept looking at one another, they needed some time alone tonight anyway.

He gave his mother a kiss and told her where he was going. She took his hand and ushered him to her bedroom.

Dex frowned, confused. Then she removed a ring box from inside the drawer of her jewelry box and handed it to him. "This was the promise ring your father first gave me when he proposed." She gestured toward the wedding ring she'd never removed. "Later he bought me a bigger diamond. You can do the same for Melissa later if you want, but for now, maybe she'd accept this."

Emotions clogged his throat. The fact that she was giving him her ring meant more to him than words. It meant she accepted Melissa into the family.

And why wouldn't she? Melissa was the most loving woman he'd ever known. She'd seen something in a stranger's eyes and trusted it when Dex had been too blind to believe. He'd lost faith…but Melissa had restored it and given him so much more.

Too emotional to speak, he thanked his mother with a kiss, then went through the kitchen and snagged a set of keys for one of the ranch work trucks from the hook by the door. Adrenaline pumping through him, he jogged outside and drove to the shelter.

Disappointment hit him when he realized Melissa wasn't there.

Maybe she'd gone home first. He spun the truck around and sped toward her house.

Time to tell her how he felt.

He just hoped she loved him in return.

TEARS BURNED THE backs of Melissa's eyelids as she tossed clothes into her suitcase. It was better this way. Better to move on and start somewhere fresh where she could forget about Dex and his family and how much she loved the darn man.

Grateful she didn't have any sentimental mementos sitting around that needed boxing up, she snatched the picture of her and her father and jammed it in her bag. Her clothes were rumpled and messy, but who cared?

She hated to leave Lend-A-Hand, but there were dozens of other shelters where she could work. Sure, she'd exhausted a few of them in Texas, but it was a big state. Maybe she'd move to the southern end. There were always people in need.

Helping others would enable her to forget about herself.

She hated needing Dex. But she did.

Tears overflowed, and she swiped at them. She'd have to be satisfied knowing she'd helped him piece his family back together again. Maybe he could finally forgive himself for his sister's death and find peace now that his father was home.

She rushed to the bathroom and tossed her makeup bag and toiletries into her toiletry case, then hurried to set it by her suitcase at the door. She was just carrying it out to her car when the sound of an engine rumbled.

She froze, one hand on the handle of her luggage as a pickup rolled into her drive. For a second, fear caught in her throat. Had Baxter sent someone after her?

But the truck engine died, and Dex slid from the truck. He looked so handsome and tall and masculine and wonderful that she almost threw herself into his arms.

But he took one look at the suitcase in her hand, and his jaw hardened. "Going somewhere?"

Her stomach clenched. "I figured it was time for me to move on."

"Why?"

Her hand was sweating so badly she dropped the suitcase with a thud against the pavement.

"Why are you leaving?" he asked.

She shrugged. "That's what I do. I help at a shelter, then after a while move to where I'm needed more."

He stared at her, emotions warring in his eyes. "What if you're needed here?"

She exhaled. "April can handle the shelter."

He stepped forward, so close she inhaled his masculine scent. Lord help her, she wanted him. "I'm not referring to the shelter."

She swallowed.

"You're running," he said boldly. "And I want to know why."

Pain knifed through her chest. "I can't stay where I don't belong," she said. "People move on."

"Not when they have people who care about them. Not when they have family."

"The people at the shelters are my family."

"It doesn't have to be that way," he said. "The Hawks care about you, Melissa. My father thinks of you like a daughter. The rest of the family is so damn grateful to you for being kind to him and bringing him back that they want you to stay, too."

She jutted her chin in the air, her chest about to explode. "I don't want your gratitude, Dex. I did what I did because that's who I am. I believed in Jim, I mean Steven, and I'm glad I did. No one needs to feel indebted for that."

"I know, you did it because you have an incredibly generous heart." He inched closer. His breath was shaky, and his lips parted, his hand trembling as he reached for hers. "And this is not about gratitude."

Hope budded in her chest. But hope was dangerous. "Then what is it about, Dex?"

He pressed a kiss to her hand, a kiss so tender that her knees nearly buckled.

"I think you're leaving because you're scared. I understand that more than you know." His breath rushed out. "I understand what it's like to feel abandoned. To shut down and close yourself off from others because you're afraid of getting hurt."

She blinked back the tears, her pulse throbbing.

"But I promise you I will never abandon you." His gaze met hers, then he dropped to his knees in front of her, removed a ring box from his pocket and held it out.

"I love you, Melissa. I want you." His voice cracked as he opened the box. A thin silver band holding an oval shaped diamond glinted back at her. "I want you to be my wife."

"Dex—"

"The ring was my mother's," he said as he removed it from the velvet interior. "It was her promise ring, and she wanted you to have it." He swallowed. "*I* want you to have it as a promise that I'll always love you, that I'll never leave you." His voice wavered. "Later, I'll buy you a bigger ring if you want. You can pick it out—"

"I don't want a big ring," she said in a raw whisper. "I don't need fancy things, Dex. All I've ever wanted was a family. And…someone to love."

"We can have that love and family together," he said gruffly. He reached for her hand again and slipped the ring on her finger. "Just say yes, that you'll be my wife."

Her heart swelled with love, and emotions overcame her. Tears streamed down her cheeks as she nodded and whispered yes.

Dex swung her into his arms and kissed her deeply, and she kissed him with all the longing and love in her heart.

She'd been running all her life, afraid to get hurt.

From now on, the only place she was running was into Dex's arms.

* * * * *

COMING NEXT MONTH FROM
Ⓗ HARLEQUIN®

INTRIGUE

Available March 19, 2019

#1845 MARINE FORCE RECON
Declan's Defenders • by Elle James
Former marine Declan O'Neill set up a vigilante task force, and his first mission involves helping Grace Lawrence find her missing roommate. Will they be able to locate the woman before her unearthed secrets endanger them all?

#1846 HER ALIBI
by Carol Ericson
Although he was once a cop, Connor Wells agrees to help Savannah Martell, the woman he has always loved, after she tells him she is being framed for her ex-husband's murder—but is he protecting a killer?

#1847 ICE COLD KILLER
Eagle Mountain Murder Mystery: Winter Storm Wedding
by Cindi Myers
A winter storm is blocking the only road in and out of Eagle Mountain, Colorado, and a serial killer is on the loose. To protect the town, State Patrol officer Ryder Stewart and grieving veterinarian Darcy Marsh will need to work together to fight an unknown assailant—and their attraction to each other.

#1848 SMOKY MOUNTAINS RANGER
The Mighty McKenzies • by Lena Diaz
When ranger Adam McKenzie sees a woman being threatened, he vows to do whatever it takes to protect her. But private investigator Jody Ingram knows nothing about the gunmen she is running from. Can Adam save Jody from the unknown forces that threaten her?

#1849 WYOMING COWBOY MARINE
Carsons & Delaneys: Battle Tested • by Nicole Helm
After Hilly Adams reports a missing person who doesn't seem to exist, Cam Delaney takes it upon himself to investigate the situation. Suddenly, people are after Hilly, and Cam must step in to protect the strange woman. Who is she... and who is the man who disappeared?

#1850 UNDERCOVER JUSTICE
by Nico Rosso
Stephanie Shun and Arash Shamshiri infiltrated a dangerous gang...but they each don't know the other is undercover. Will the truth about their identities bring them together or tear them apart?

HICNM0319

Get 4 FREE REWARDS!

We'll send you 2 FREE Books plus 2 FREE Mystery Gifts.

Harlequin Intrigue® books feature heroes and heroines that confront and survive danger while finding themselves irresistibly drawn to one another.

FREE
Value Over
$20

YES! Please send me 2 FREE Harlequin Intrigue® novels and my 2 FREE gifts (gifts are worth about $10 retail). After receiving them, if I don't wish to receive any more books, I can return the shipping statement marked "cancel." If I don't cancel, I will receive 6 brand-new novels every month and be billed just $4.99 each for the regular-print edition or $5.74 each for the larger-print edition in the U.S., or $5.74 each for the regular-print edition or $6.49 each for the larger-print edition in Canada. That's a savings of at least 12% off the cover price! It's quite a bargain! Shipping and handling is just 50¢ per book in the U.S. and 75¢ per book in Canada.* I understand that accepting the 2 free books and gifts places me under no obligation to buy anything. I can always return a shipment and cancel at any time. The free books and gifts are mine to keep no matter what I decide.

Choose one: ☐ **Harlequin Intrigue®**
Regular-Print
(182/382 HDN GMYW)

☐ **Harlequin Intrigue®**
Larger-Print
(199/399 HDN GMYW)

Name (please print)

Address   Apt. #

City   State/Province   Zip/Postal Code

Mail to the **Reader Service:**
IN U.S.A.: P.O. Box 1341, Buffalo, NY 14240-8531
IN CANADA: P.O. Box 603, Fort Erie, Ontario L2A 5X3

Want to try 2 free books from another series? Call 1-800-873-8635 or visit www.ReaderService.com.

SPECIAL EXCERPT FROM

⊕ HARLEQUIN®

I N T R I G U E

*Former marine Declan O'Neill is building an
organization to protect people who can't defend
themselves. Grace Lawrence wants to find her
roommate, and Declan is the only one who will help her.
With Grace's tireless search putting her in the line of
fire, can Declan save both women before it's too late?*

Read on for a sneak preview of
Marine Force Recon
by New York Times *and* USA TODAY *bestselling
author Elle James.*

Declan O'Neill hiked his rucksack higher on his shoulders
and trudged down the sidewalk in downtown Washington,
DC. The last time he'd seen so many people in one place,
he'd been a fresh recruit at US Marine Corps basic training
in San Diego, California, standing among a bunch of
teenagers, just like him, being processed into the military.

He shouldered his way through the throngs of
sightseers, businessmen and career women hurrying to the
next building along the road. The sun shone on a bright
spring day. Cherry blossoms exploded in fluffy pinkish-
white, dripping petals onto the lawns and sidewalks in an
optimistic display of hope.

Hope.

Declan snorted. Here he was, eleven years after joining
the US Marine Corps…eleven years of knowing what was
expected of him, of not having to decide what to wear each
day. Eleven years of a steady paycheck, no matter how

small, in an honorable profession, making a difference in the world.

Now he was faced with the daunting task of job hunting with a huge strike on his record.

But not today.

Why he'd decided to take the train from Bethesda, Maryland, to the political hub of the entire country was beyond his own comprehension. But with nowhere else to go and nothing holding him back—no job, no family, no home—he'd thought, "Why not?"

He'd never been to the White House, never stopped to admire the Declaration of Independence, drafted by the forefathers of his country and he'd never stood at the foot of the Lincoln Memorial, in the shadow of the likeness of Abraham Lincoln, a leader who'd set the United States on a revolutionary course. He'd never been to the Vietnam War Memorial or any other memorial in DC.

Yeah. And so what?

Sightseeing wouldn't pay the bills. Out of the military, out of money and sporting a dishonorable discharge, Declan would be hard-pressed to find a decent job. Who would hire a man whose only skills were superb marksmanship that allowed him to kill a man from four hundred yards away, expertise in hand-to-hand combat and the ability to navigate himself out of a paper bag with nothing more than the stars and his wits?

Don't miss
Marine Force Recon *by Elle James,*
available April 2019 wherever
Harlequin® Intrigue books and ebooks are sold.

www.Harlequin.com

SPECIAL EXCERPT FROM

H◆I
HQN™

A blizzard is keeping guests at Sterling Montana Guest Ranch, where a killer is lurking in the shadows.

Read on for a sneak preview of
Stroke of Luck *by* New York Times *and* USA TODAY *bestselling author B.J. Daniels.*

"Bad luck always comes in threes."

Standing in the large kitchen of the Sterling Montana Guest Ranch, Will Sterling shot the woman an impatient look. "I don't have time for this right now, Dorothea."

"Just sayin'," Dorothea Brand muttered under her breath. The fifty-year-old housekeeper was short and stout with a helmet of dark hair and piercing dark eyes. She'd been a fixture on the ranch since Will and his brothers were kids, which made her invaluable, but also as bossy as an old mother hen.

After the Sterling boys had lost their mother, Dorothea had stepped in. Their father, Wyatt, had continued to run the guest ranch alone and then with the help of his sons until his death last year. For the first time, Will would finally be running the guest ranch without his father calling all the shots. He'd been looking forward to the challenge and to carrying on the family business.

But now his cook was laid up with a broken leg? He definitely didn't like the way the season was starting, Will thought as the housekeeper leaned against the counter, giving him one of her you're-going-to-regret-this looks as he considered who he could call.

As his brother Garrett brought in a box of supplies from town, Will asked, "Do you know anyone who can cook?"

"What about Poppy Carmichael?" Garrett suggested as he pulled a bottle of water from the refrigerator, opened it and took a long drink. "She's a caterer now."

PHBJDEXP0319

Will frowned. "Poppy?" An image appeared of a girl with freckles, braces, skinned knees and reddish-brown hair in pigtails. "I haven't thought of Poppy in years. I thought she moved away."

"She did, but she came back about six months ago and started a catering business in Whitefish," Garrett said. "I only know because I ran into her at a party recently. The food was really good, if that helps."

"Wait, I remember her. Cute kid. Didn't her father work for the forest service?" their younger brother Shade asked as he also came into the kitchen with a box of supplies. He deposited the box inside the large pantry just off the kitchen. "Last box," he announced, dusting off his hands.

"You remember, Will. Poppy and her dad lived in the old forest service cabin a mile or so from here," Garrett said, grinning at him. "She used to ride her bike over here and help us with our chores. At least, that was her excuse."

Will avoided his brother's gaze. It wasn't like he'd ever forgotten.

"I just remember the day she decided to ride Lightning," Shade said. "She climbed up on the corral, and as the horse ran by, she jumped on it!" He shook his head, clearly filled with admiration. "I can't imagine what she thought she was going to do, riding him bareback." He laughed. "She stayed on a lot longer than I thought she would. But it's a wonder she didn't kill herself. The girl had grit. But I always wondered what possessed her to do that."

Garrett laughed and shot another look at Will. "She was trying to impress our brother."

"That poor little girl was smitten," Dorothea agreed as she narrowed her dark gaze at Will. "And you, being fifteen and full of yourself, often didn't give her the time of day. So what could possibly go wrong hiring her to cook for you?"

Don't miss
Stroke of Luck *by B.J. Daniels, available March 2019 wherever HQN Books and ebooks are sold.*

www.Harlequin.com

PHBJDEXP0319

Love Harlequin romance?

DISCOVER.

Be the first to find out about promotions, news and exclusive content!

 Facebook.com/HarlequinBooks

 Twitter.com/HarlequinBooks

 Instagram.com/HarlequinBooks

 Pinterest.com/HarlequinBooks

ReaderService.com

EXPLORE.

Sign up for the Harlequin e-newsletter and download a free book from any series at **TryHarlequin.com.**

CONNECT.

Join our Harlequin community to share your thoughts and connect with other romance readers!
Facebook.com/groups/HarlequinConnection

HARLEQUIN®

ROMANCE WHEN YOU NEED IT

HSOCIAL2018